Tarzan

and THE LOST SAFARI

Featuring the famous Tarzan created by
Edgar Rice Burroughs

Adapted from the
TARZAN motion picture

Illustrations by
TONY SGROI

Authorized Edition

WHITMAN PUBLISHING COMPANY
Racine, Wisconsin

CONTENTS

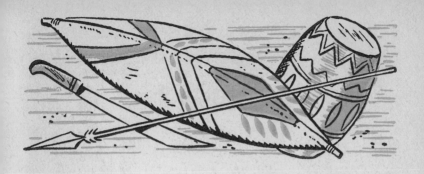

Chapter 1   **Giant in the Trees**

Giant ground ferns, head-high, vividly green in this thick jungle and massed beside a well-worn game trail that Tarzan was investigating, quivered just a little. Tarzan saw that movement, thirty feet or so ahead of him, without seeming to do so, and kept moving toward the ferns with no change in his easy, springy pace.

But, midway in a long stride, he considered and rejected a dozen reasons to explain why those ferns had quivered. Meanwhile, all his senses alertly probed for the true reason.

The time was late afternoon of a hot day. Not a breath of breeze stirred. Deep quiet in the jungle indicated that its myriad inhabitants had sought shaded spots and were drowsily waiting for night. Even the monkeys, those busybodies of the treetops, were silent.

Thinking of these things, Tarzan's ears caught a faint,

shuffling sound, feet moving against hard ground as someone shifted position deep in the mass of greenery. In the
same instant his nostrils caught an odor of human sweat
in the hot air. Together, they told who lay in wait for him
behind those ferns . . . the most dangerous of animals—man.

Out of the ferns flashed a spear, hard-thrown, aimed with
deadly accuracy at Tarzan's legs. But Tarzan was not there.
He had vanished.

The fearsomely painted and scarred bronze warrior who
had thrown the spear now leaped out of the ferns, with
a deep-throated shout: *"M-tu zanje!"* Then he halted, gog-
gling in disbelief. The man he had confidently expected to
down with his spear had vanished, like a puff of smoke.

Other warriors came crashing from the jungle, pouring
onto the game trail, until ten of them milled there. An
excited gabble of talk began. And, thirty feet above them,
Tarzan listened and watched.

There had been nothing particularly mysterious about
his disappearance. He had gone into the trees—a spring
and a catch of a limb, a twist and thrust of powerful sinewy
muscles as he leaped for another limb. In a fraction of a
second he had vanished in the jungle forest, moving upward faster than a trained athlete could climb a stepladder,

then swinging from that tree to another, from there to still another until he was above the warriors milling on the game trail.

A stir and rustling and crackling of twigs; Chetah, his chimpanzee companion on many a jungle trek, came flying to join him. She—just back from some excursion of her own —now chattered and bounced up and down, banging knuckles against bark, peering excitedly at those below.

Tarzan murmured softly, "Quiet, little one." He wanted to hear what the warriors were saying, wanted to know their tribe and what they were doing here.

The one who had thrown the spear was shouting angrily. *"M-tu zanje!"* he exclaimed again. *M-tu* was Swahili for man, and *zanje* was a word from the Ivory Coast, meaning white. And the rest of the words that came pouring from him were a mixture of East African languages, all familiar to Tarzan.

"I swear by the blood gods, it was a white man!" he cried. "Big and black-haired, browned by the sun; his one weapon was a knife, and he wore only a leopard skin."

One of those listening laughed harshly. "Who ever saw a white man like that in the jungle? You slept and dreamed it all, when you were supposed to be watching the trail while we others rested! That is what happened."

"No! I was not asleep!"

The wicked iron point of the spear he had thrown was deeply imbedded in the trunk of a giant oil palm. It was a war spear, not made for hunting.

The warriors were all big men, well muscled, all with the same bronze-colored skin. Some of them carried spears also, and long oval shields—hardwood frames covered by tightly stretched rhino hide. Several had short horn bows, with arrow quivers slung over their shoulders. Two carried old trade muskets.

A tough outfit, and primed for trouble, made even tougher in appearance by the paint daubed on them—red and blue and ocher—and by the scars on their faces and chests from ceremonial carvings they had undergone. Civilized tribes no longer practiced that barbaric custom. But here, in the remote region where Kenya merged with Ethiopia, Africa was still primitive and savage.

Who were they? Not Masai or Watusi or Kikuyu; men from those tribes would have darker skins and would be speaking their own tribal languages. That these men spoke mostly Swahili did not mean much of anything. Swahili was an artificial language, with words borrowed from many tongues, and was spoken all over East Africa.

An argument was going on now. Some were taking the side of the spear-thrower; others were still claiming he had gone to sleep and had been dreaming.

Then one who had stayed silent until now, frowning as he listened, harshly interrupted: *"Barak!* Keep quiet, all of you! We sound like old women, and not warriors who have survived the ordeal of the seven days of torture!"

He was obviously the chief of this party. And he went on, "Scatter and search through the jungle. We will find the white man, if there is one, and capture him to take with us. That is why we are here, to capture whites for sacrifice to the blood gods, so take him alive, with no more wild spear-throwing. And if we do not find a white man—" he scowled at the spear-thrower "—you will not return with us. But your head will. I myself will throw it in the pit of skulls at Opar!"

Tarzan grunted, deep in his great chest. Now he knew who they were—Oparian warriors. And the things their leader had said told Tarzan he had at last come upon something in the search that had led him so far across Africa.

But this was not the end of that search. He had only arrived at a starting point. Now he must trail them, follow along wherever they went, until they returned to their fabled, hidden city of Opar. This was Tarzan's goal, his reason for being here. He had to find Opar.

Meanwhile, having learned all he needed to know, Tarzan glanced around, ready to move away, find some safer spot from which to watch the Oparian warriors.

And Chetah, who had remained silent for several minutes, an intolerably long time for her, suddenly grimaced and chattered, broke off a branch and threw it down, hitting one of those below on the head.

The Oparians looked up. They saw Chetah—and they also saw Tarzan!

For a frozen instant, none of them moved, all staring in disbelief at the giant white man above their heads, thirty feet up, balanced on a wide, jutting limb of a towering hagenia tree.

Tarzan seized upon that moment. Chetah had revealed him to them, and there was nothing to be gained by fretting about that. But he could let them know the manner of man they had talked about capturing.

And he did, with a clenched fist that beat against his chest half a dozen times, a drumming tattoo of sound like a rumble of thunder. Then his challenging cry rang far across the jungle, deep-toned, piercing, rising and falling, a chant that was at once a battle cry and a warning:

"*Ah—ee—ahhhhhh!*"

It awoke the drowsing monkeys in the treetops to squalling, frightened frenzy. Distantly, a lone bull elephant trumpeted an answer. From nearer at hand came the coughing roars of lions. A hyena, that outcast of the animal kingdom, sounded its maniac laughter of fear.

A second passed. The echoes of Tarzan's cry began to come back. Then those below shook off their spell of frozen disbelief. Their spears came hissing up at him, an effort to wound and bring him down. Bow strings twanged loudly and arrows whistled in flight, clawing for him with their barbed points. Those who had muskets fired them.

But again Tarzan was not there. He had turned and leaped far into space, reaching for and gripping a tough liana, a long, ropelike vine twining itself through the trees. He swung on this, let go and hurled himself up and out again, high above the ground, moving away almost faster than a man's eye could follow him.

The thickly massed trees of the jungle had been a highway for Tarzan ever since he had been a child raised by the great apes in another jungle more than a thousand miles away. Traveling at a speed faster than a man could run, instinctively judging—while hurtling through space—the strength of branches and vines ahead he meant to use, covering forty feet or more with some of his leaps, he drew quickly beyond range of the Oparians' weapons.

But he kept on for several miles, climbing steadily upward as he moved, until he was literally running through the tops of trees that towered three hundred feet above the jungle floor. This was mostly for the sheer love of it, an outpouring of all the energy bottled up in him during the time he had spent today earth-bound, working along the game trail, reading its tracks, seeking some sign of man. He had found none. The Oparians had come from the other direction.

Tarzan stopped after a while, swaying easily on a lofty perch that gave him a wide view. Those Oparians would not—could not—move very quickly from the spot where he had seen them. Presently he would go back to start trailing that party of ten warriors, beginning the patient watch that must continue until they returned to their city —Opar, home of the legendary ivory hoard.

And also—Opar, the place of a bloodthirsty sort of cruelty that must be stamped out at once.

Tarzan remembered a moment many days ago at a native village far from here, and the words of a young Englishman who was district commissioner for this area, a region much larger than England itself.

"Five white men disappeared from my district last year, including the chap before me in this job," the commissioner had said. "Since coming here I have heard ugly rumors that they were captured and taken to Opar, sacrificed to pagan gods there. I would like to investigate the rumor; find Opar, if the place really exists; bring the murderers to justice, if those whites were actually sacrificed. But I have only about a dozen *askaris*—native soldiers—and because of the Mau Mau trouble I have to stay here."

Mau Maus were fanatic members of a secret society among the Kikuyu who killed natives and whites alike. They had turned most of Kenya into an armed camp.

Tarzan had heard of Opar. Who in Africa had not? It was said to be somewhere in the towering mountains that were just over the wild southern border of Ethiopia, the home of the ivory hoard—giant elephant tusks piled high in a hidden cave, collected for hundreds of years.

Tarzan had no interest in ivory treasure. But white men being sacrificed to pagan gods—this was something that had to be stopped at once, if true. And so, instead of returning to his own hundred-thousand-acre estate in the hardwood forests along the Ruwenzori River, he had plunged into the jungle, on a search that had been fruitless until this day.

Chetah now came along to join him on his high, swaying treetop. She, who looked so clumsy on the ground with her short legs and long arms, could move through the upper reaches almost as fast as Tarzan, though she preferred to ride on his back and was grumbling because he had not waited for her to do so.

"Do not scold me," Tarzan said, with mock severity. "Instead, you are the one who should be scolded. You should not have thrown that branch. You have been bad."

Chetah had a rudimentary language of her own, made up of squeaks and grunts, that Tarzan could speak if he wished. She also understood a great many English words, and knew quite well what "bad" meant. The chimpanzee ducked her head, lifted both forearms to cover her face, and mumbled apologetically.

"I forgive you," Tarzan said. "Now you are good again, but probably not for long. And—" he lifted himself, balancing on his precarious perch "—it is time for us to go back, find those Oparians again—"

The words died in his throat. For a moment, head tilted up, he forgot about the Oparians as he scanned the sky.

A sound had reached him, a distant buzzing that increased quickly in volume.

Hand shading his eyes against the brilliant sun, he looked and found, almost at once, far off to southward, a tiny dot that quickly increased in size against the blue vault of heaven.

"A plane!" Tarzan muttered. "What is it doing here?"

No commercial plane flew even an irregular schedule across this corner of Africa. There were no landing fields, no supplies of petrol available. The jet liners followed a course well to westward of here, spanning the distance from Cairo to Johannesburg in one giant leap.

Perhaps an R.A.F. patrol ship? But Tarzan shook his head. He could make out the approaching craft now, at a distance when it would still be only a dot to anyone else. "That's a private plane," he said aloud. "A two-engine craft, perhaps a Moth or an Avion."

Such planes, he knew, flew out of Nairobi, the big-game hunting capital of Africa. They were chartered by wealthy sportsmen to reach good shooting areas in a hurry.

Nairobi was many hundreds of miles to the south and east. What such a plane was doing this far from its home base, venturing over country that was still largely only a blank space on the map, was an interesting question. But only those aboard it knew the answer. Tarzan shrugged, starting to turn away.

Chetah asked a hopeful question, and he nodded. She sprang to his back, feet digging in and hands gripping his shoulders. Chetah was grinning with joy. She liked nothing more than flying through space with Tarzan doing all the work.

He said, "Hold on tight!" But then he paused.

Some intuition made Tarzan glance upward at the plane again. He frowned. "It's in trouble!"

A thin streamer of black smoke had suddenly appeared, trailing out behind one of the two motors, whose smooth rhythm now became jerky and ragged. The plane veered down, beginning to lose altitude as it made a wide turn that brought it in Tarzan's direction.

He cried, "Keep its nose up or you'll crash!"

The pilot was fighting hard, but vainly, to do that—to hold altitude. The plane swept over Tarzan and Chetah, heading west, that streamer of smoke thick and black, the

propeller now not turning at all. And suddenly smoke began to spew from the other engine, also.

Chetah pounded impatiently against Tarzan's back. She had seen and heard man-birds before. This one did not interest her. She wanted a piggyback ride through the trees.

Off in the distance the plane yawed heavily, struggling in a wide turn, and started to come back.

Tarzan moved now. He leaped out and down, with a suddenness and speed that made Chetah squeal in fright and dig her fingers into the thick, hard muscles of his back. A one-handed catch of a vine and he hurtled across a wide arc of space, a leap at the end carrying him even farther.

A twist of Tarzan's head showed him the plane again. It was at stalling speed, settling inexorably toward the trees. He measured an angle that showed him where it was likely to come down, and hurried on, heading toward that spot —though it appeared likely that no one could hope to land in jungle such as this and survive.

The plane struggled past, overhead, no more than a hundred feet above the treetops. Both engines were now silent. The pilot, realizing he could not keep his craft in the air, had cut his switches, in an effort at least to avoid the danger of fire.

Suddenly, and quite surprisingly, the jungle thinned out. Looking ahead, Tarzan saw a break in the land, a dark line that was a slash in the earth. It was one of the volcanic canyons that were frequent in this area, formed by some convulsion ages ago. The Great Rift of Kenya, south of here, which extended clear across the Red Sea into Arabia, was the best known of them.

This canyon ahead was much narrower than the Great Rift, but still was at least a quarter of a mile wide. And for another quarter of a mile or so on both sides of it there was little jungle growth, few trees.

Tarzan understood now why the pilot of the plane had turned and headed back. He had sighted the relatively clear space this side of the canyon and would try to land.

Knowing something of planes, Tarzan did not think the effort would succeed. He left the trees, a dizzying descent that ended with a long swing that left him running along the ground, breaking from the jungle, as the plane's wheels touched the earth.

It raced on, fast—too fast—lurching and swaying. One of its wings sheared off a sturdy thorn-tree sapling, then seemed only to touch a great black boulder jutting from the earth. But that impact was enough to fold the wing back against the fuselage like crumpled cardboard.

Another boulder ripped off the undercarriage. One of the engines was torn away and bounced like a basketball, flying eventually into the canyon.

All of this with an earsplitting succession of sounds that woke the jungle again, as Tarzan's call had awakened it previously. Now the pilot saw the canyon ahead and tried desperately to turn his crippled craft. It slid on sideways, losing some momentum as it smashed through more boulders that tore away metal in long strips.

Tarzan was running at his top speed, a long, reaching stride; he had shaken Chetah off on reaching the ground. She scrambled along after him with plaintive cries, begging that he wait for her.

The plane smashed into a rocky ledge about five feet high, near the very edge of the canyon, slid over that and down on the ledge's far side—then stopped.

For only a second, though. Then it tilted slowly sideways toward the canyon and began to slide again. Its unbroken wing tilted upward, toward Tarzan. Nothing, he thought, could keep it from going on over, falling into the canyon, with probable death for all inside. And he was still about a hundred yards away.

Chapter 2   On the Canyon's Edge

The wing stopped its upward tilt and very slowly dipped down again until it rested against the ground.

Tarzan ran through the cloud of dust that had been stirred up by the plane's long slide to the edge of the canyon. He leaped over the rocky ledge and paused for a quick glance down into that gash in the earth. It had sheer rock walls and was at least a hundred feet deep.

The plane was balanced precariously at its very edge. If the wing on that side had not been crumpled against the fuselage, its extended weight would probably have pulled the craft on over, and down to destruction. Tarzan felt it was likely the plane would still go into the gorge. Chance had stopped it only inches short of doing so; it could still slide those few inches.

He moved quickly along the fuselage, toward a door

just this side of the still intact wing. Beside the door was a round window. Tarzan saw a face pressed against the glass—wide, frightened eyes that grew wider still as they sighted him, pallid features reflecting fear that must be close to hysteria.

"A woman!" The exclamation was jolted from him. That a woman was in the plane made it even more imperative that he work fast before the craft plummeted into the canyon.

The door had a jutting handle. Tarzan grasped this, but found it would not turn. He shook it hard. From within the plane a man's muffled voice reached him: "—it's jammed! Won't open!"

Tarzan gripped firmly, using both hands. The great muscles in his arms and back bulged like steel cables. He put all his strength against the door and ripped it open, with a rending crash of metal fittings tearing loose. Tarzan had literally wrenched the door completely out of its frame.

A man appeared before him, started to crowd out of the plane. Tarzan put a hand against his chest, shoving him back. "Let the woman come first."

"Huh?" He was a big fellow with arrogant features. "Who do you think you are, to be giving me orders?"

Then he had a good look at Tarzan, and his voice trailed off. A first glimpse of the jungle giant frequently had this effect on people. The man muttered sullenly, "Well, all right. Come on, Camage, get out of here. And hurry it up, will you?"

The woman Tarzan had glimpsed appeared in the doorway. She was quite plump, with a round face and full cheeks; she wore a white linen jacket and skirt, and the plane's crash had terrified her almost out of her wits. "I—I'm afraid! Hal, help me, please!"

"Get out of here!" The man gave her a rough shove. She would have fallen to the ground if Tarzan had not caught her.

"Climb up on that rock ledge, please," he said. "The plane might still go over, and that wing will sweep around if it does—"

She shrank from him as though he were a ghost, eyes bulging, a hand up to her mouth.

The man came out now, scrambling past the woman and climbing up on the ledge.

Another man appeared, leaping down, a thin, stringy fellow who wore a white hunter's hat and carried a rifle. He stared also in amazement at Tarzan, but with a grunt of recognition. "Tarzan! What are *you* doing here?"

Tarzan remembered him with distaste. "Hawkins, you're a long way from your usual stamping grounds."

Josiah Hawkins went at the ledge and up it, also.

Tarzan glanced at the plump woman. "Anybody else inside?"

She did not answer, but goggled at him, frozen where she stood. Tarzan unceremoniously picked her up, lifted her to the ledge. "One of you men look after this lady."

The man she had called Hal reluctantly pulled her to safety. Tarzan turned again to the plane, as another woman came out.

This one also wore bush jacket and linen skirt. She was rather tall and pretty, but with a petulant look about her. Pausing in the doorway, she studied Tarzan with lifted brows. "My word! Our guardian angel turns out to be an African Hercules in a leopard skin!"

Her voice was an affected, supercilious drawl. Her entire manner was in striking contrast to the fear of the plump woman, but Tarzan sensed that this one was just as frightened inwardly, but determined not to show her fear. He reached up, lifted her down and clear of the plane.

The woman's lips parted in a stiff sort of smile. "You're

quite strong, mister. But what are you doing here at this back end of nowhere? I'd as soon expect to see a Zulu in Central Park, New York—"

Tarzan interrupted her: "Are there any more in the plane?"

"Why, I don't think so." She glanced up at those on the ledge. "Camage, Hal Fletcher, Hawkins—" Then, with a sudden fearful cry, "Dick isn't there! He must still be inside!"

She turned and started back toward the gaping door. Tarzan stopped her. "Get up on the ledge. I'll go in after him."

Fingers clawed anxiously at her lips. "Please h-hurry. He's my husband!"

Tarzan swung himself lithely through the door, and with care. He paused a second, accustoming his vision to the dimmer light within, and in that second felt the plane slide sideways a little, toward the canyon, with a grating sound. Tarzan's lips tightened. He looked forward.

He stood in a small cabin, paneled with brightly polished mahogany. There was a deep, soft rug underfoot. Tarzan saw two leather lounging chairs and a divan, all bolted to the floor. This craft, poised on the brink of destruction, had been luxuriously outfitted for its ill-fated flight.

The pilot's cubicle, forward, had been closed off from the cabin by a bulkhead and a door. Tarzan heard a muffled thump, and a pounding from the far side of the door. He went to it, keeping his weight away from the canyon side of the plane.

Again he had to tear a door out of its frame; this one was jammed, also. But the task was easier. One jerk was enough to rip it open. Tarzan saw a dark-haired young man, attired in gray flannel trousers and a shirt of rough cotton weave, who swayed unsteadily. He had a small cut across his forehead and a trickle of blood down the side of his face.

"Thanks, whoever you are," he muttered. "Must have been knocked out at the last—came to and found I couldn't get that door open. I'm still dizzy—"

He sagged toward Tarzan, who picked him up bodily and went back through the cabin.

The plane slid toward the canyon edge again. Tarzan ran at the cabin door and leaped through it. He fell as he did so—deliberately, slamming the man that he carried flat against the ground and then hugging it beside him.

The plane's wing came whipping around, barely clear-

ing them. The plane slid over the canyon rim. And a screaming of ripping metal began as it plummeted down the sheer rock wall, capped by a thunderous roar as it crashed at the bottom.

Tarzan stood up again. Another pall of dust eddied about him, but a late afternoon breeze that now began to blow whipped it quickly away.

The man at his feet was pushing himself up, shaking his head to clear it. Tarzan studied him and then the four on the rock ledge.

Two white women and three white men, stranded here in this wildest, most savage corner of Africa, the nearest outpost of civilization many days of arduous travel distant.

And very nearby a party of Oparian warriors was hunting for whites to sacrifice to pagan gods.

Tarzan went to the canyon edge for a look at the plane. It had struck nose down and had broken in half, with the tail assembly tearing away. Both sections of the plane now seemed to be twisted, broken wreckage.

Chetah, left behind during that race from the fringe of the jungle, had reached the canyon edge and now jumped up and down, chattering with excitement, peering into the gorge at the ruined plane and demanding what all of this meant.

"I don't know. Let's both go and find out," Tarzan told her, and turned to the five who were grouped together on the low stone ledge.

The pretty young woman was talking, voice raised in petulant anger: "—all your fault, Dick! You checked that plane at Nairobi, and said it was all right then—"

"Diana, please!" It was the young man with the cut on his forehead. He sounded very tired. "Nobody can ever anticipate a broken oil line. It was completely an accident—"

"Well, you could certainly have done something to fix it, instead of dumping us in this awful place!"

They fell silent then, as Tarzan moved toward them. The young man came to meet him, hand outstretched.

"You saved my life. I'm very grateful. My name is Dick Penrod. May I present my wife, Diana, and her companion, Camage Dean—" He was referring to the plump woman, who again shrank back. She was, Tarzan realized, afraid of him. Dick Penrod continued, "That is Hal Fletcher—" the fellow who had tried to leave the plane first, and who now looked Tarzan over with a supercilious lift of his lip.

"And Josiah Hawkins." Dick Penrod paused a second, then added, "Hawkins has told us—er—something about you—"

The man couldn't have had time to tell very much, Tarzan thought—probably that he was a white savage who lived in the jungle and about whom strange tales were told, and possibly that he might prove helpful.

As for Josiah Hawkins, Tarzan knew all about him: a one-time safari guide who had been kicked out of the White Hunters' Association at Nairobi for illegal elephant-shooting, and who had been arrested several times for ivory-poaching. He was suspected of having sold guns to the Mau Mau terrorists in Kenya and of having been engaged in the brutal traffic that still smuggled kidnaped natives out of Africa and across the Red Sea to slavery in Arabia.

A thoroughly unsavory person, all in all, Josiah Hawkins was not to be trusted for a minute, in anything.

Tarzan spoke bluntly: "What are you people doing here?"

They were all silent for a moment. It was Hal Fletcher, the big fellow with the arrogant attitude, who spoke first. "I'd say that is no particular business of yours," he told Tarzan, with an even more pronounced curl of his lip.

"You're right, Hal," Diana Penrod agreed. "Just be-

cause he happened to be wandering around in this neighborhood when we crashed doesn't give him the right to
ask us impertinent questions."

"Oh, Diana, you shouldn't talk like that," Dick Penrod
protested. "If it hadn't been for him, we might all have
been killed."

"What do you know about it?" his young wife snapped
at him. "I'm sure there would have been time for all
of us to have gotten out of the plane, even if he hadn't
been here."

Camage Dean, the plump woman, spoke hesitantly:
"He—he got the side door open when Hal couldn't—"

"Shut up, Camage," Diana ordered brusquely. "As usual,
you were too scared to know what was going on."

"I'd have had that door open with one more shove," Hal
Fletcher said. "I agree with you, Diana, we don't owe this
muscle-bound character anything. And we can make out
fine now without him. Why doesn't somebody tell him to
beat it?"

"Well, I couldn't have gotten the door open that was
keeping me in the plane," Dick Penrod said. "He saved
my life, at least. And I'm going to tell him what he wants
to know—"

"Dick, you'll do no such thing!" Diana cried.

"I think it's advisable," Penrod said stubbornly. He faced Tarzan, "We four—Diana, Camage, Fletcher, and myself—went to Nairobi for some big-game hunting. But Diana grew bored after only a couple of days, and wanted to try something different. Then Hawkins came along. After he talked to Diana, she insisted we return to Nairobi, where she bought that plane. Then we flew north in it."

Tarzan stared at him, puzzled, then at Hawkins. "There's plenty of big game hereabouts," he said, "but you couldn't go after it without native beaters, gun-boys, trucks, camping equipment. And there's no place anywhere in this area for safe landing of a plane—"

"We didn't mean to hunt big game," Penrod said. "Hawkins told us about a native city in mountain country where we could land and get out again. He said the natives there have a lot of prime old ivory—that we could trade with them for all the plane would carry, then fly on to Djibouti, sell it to Indian merchants and make an enormous profit—"

Tarzan interrupted him: "Hawkins, were you talking to these people about Opar?"

The lanky man had a prompt answer: "Sure! I've been there. Know the chief very well—Ogonooroo, a stupid old fool. Show him some flashy trinkets, he'd give plenty of ivory for them. I saw the tusks, too, all piled up in a cave, some of them hundreds of years old and twenty feet long. You know what old ivory like that would bring, for the Indian market?"

Tarzan knew. India was the world's greatest user of ivory. The Hindu religion required it for many ceremonial objects. Tusks such as Hawkins had described would bring an enormous price, for shipment to India.

But would people such as the warriors he had seen a while ago trade their ivory off for flashy trinkets? Tarzan greatly doubted it. And the thought of these white people going to Opar, where whites were desired for blood sacrifice, turned him cold.

"Anything wrong with my plan?" Hawkins challenged.

Tarzan had a strange feeling that the man had been telling at least part of the truth, that he actually had been to Opar. If so, he must be the only white man alive who could say that.

"Yes," Tarzan answered. "You might possibly have made it to Opar, but your plane's gas tanks would have been empty, or nearly so, when you landed."

"No, they wouldn't," Hawkins said. "Dar-es-Said, up

in the Sudan, has a landing field, and you can buy petrol there. We meant to fly to Dar-es-Said, fill our tanks, then go on to Opar. After loading the ivory, it would have been an easy hop down to Djibouti on the Indian Ocean."

Perhaps there actually was a landing field at Dar-es-Said; Tarzan did not know. And it could be that Hawkins actually had believed in the weird, impractical-sounding scheme he had outlined.

That did not matter, however. The plan had failed. These five had become jungle castaways. And they could not linger here. The Oparian warriors must have seen the plane and heard it crash. They might be widely spread out through the jungle, hunting Tarzan, but that could not be counted on. They might also be converging on this spot to investigate.

These people had to be hurried away from here. A camp of some sort had to be made. They had to be fed. After those things were done, Tarzan could then consider what was to be done about them next.

But before he could announce his decision, Diana Penrod spoke again.

"So you know all about us," she said, with an angry glance at her husband. "And I really don't think you deserve much thanks for what you did, but I'll offer them, anyway. Now you can go along."

With difficulty Tarzan repressed an impulse to laugh. He kept his face wooden as he said, "And just what are you going to do?"

"Oh, we'll make out all right. The men can climb down into that canyon and get our supplies out of the plane. We'll make a camp here for tonight. Tomorrow we'll go on, walking. It will be tiresome, of course, thanks to Dick and his stupidity in letting the plane crash, and it will take us a little longer to get to Opar—"

Tarzan pointed toward the east, interrupting her: "Do you see that thin blue line against the horizon? Those are the mountains of Ethiopia. Opar is somewhere in them. You might make it to the mountains in about five days, if you walk—and if you aren't bitten by one of a dozen varieties of poisonous snakes, if you aren't charged and trampled by a bull elephant, a buffalo, or a rhino, or mauled by leopards—"

Diana sniffed. "I'm sure you're exaggerating. Hawkins can protect us with his rifle."

"No, he can't. That isn't an express rifle, but a light-caliber Mannlicher. An elephant wouldn't even feel a bullet from it. But there's a much better reason why things aren't going to be as you are planning."

"What reason?" she demanded.

"Go take a look at the walls of that canyon," Tarzan said. "None of you can possibly get down them to the plane. You'll only break your necks if you try."

Diana chewed her lip, looking baffled—but only for a moment.

"Very well, then; you'll provide the supplies we need!" she said. "I think that will be best, anyway. Take us along to your place at once. I'm tired and hungry. I would like a hot bath and a good dinner—and I do hope you'll dress properly when we all sit down at your table! Yes, that will be the best solution, all the way around. You can also provide us with native bearers, adequately armed of course, so that the dangers you mentioned won't bother us. I'll pay you well, by bank draft when we reach Djibouti."

Tarzan had to smile. Diana Penrod obviously had money, probably a great deal of it, and maybe this was the reason her husband accepted her scornful attitude toward him. She had been raised in the belief she could buy anything. Perhaps this was the first time in her life that she couldn't.

"What's the matter?" Diana demanded sharply. "You

do have a place to live, don't you?"

"Yes," Tarzan answered, and for a moment thought of his forest home in the Congo highlands beside the Ruwen-zori River, where he lived the wild, free life he had known during his years among the great apes, accepting from civil-ization only the things that meant peace and plenty for his native friends—occasionally, as on the trek that had led him by chance to that young district commissioner, wan-dering restlessly far across Africa.

"The place where I live is many days from here," he told Diana. "I have no supplies, only this knife." And he touched it, a six-inch-broad blade of Sheffield steel, thrust into a sheath over his leopard skin. "As far as I know, the nearest natives are more than a hundred miles away. The nearest house and the nearest white man are farther than that."

There was no need to mention the Oparian warriors, unless and until necessity compelled him to do so.

Diana Penrod's face went completely pale. She looked toward the canyon and moistened her lips, tried to speak but could not. Now she, and the others, fully understood the perilous predicament confronting them.

Dick Penrod studied Tarzan with a wondering frown,

trying to comprehend this man who lived as he pleased, his home the jungle, needing only the knife at his side, wanting nothing more.

Camage Dean seemed in a daze. Hal Fletcher rubbed his face and suddenly turned to Hawkins—with the thought, Tarzan told himself, that Hawkins and his rifle might insure Fletcher, at least, a chance to get back to civilization, no matter what happened to the others.

But Hawkins backed away from him. It was plain that the lanky man was for Josiah Hawkins first, last, and all the time. If anybody got out of this predicament, his attitude said, it would be Hawkins. Fletcher could look after himself.

Diana at last found her voice: "We can't stay here in this h-horrible place!" she cried. "What are we going to do?"

The sun was setting. Nearby a jackal barked yappingly, and a lion sounded its deep, hungry roar. Even closer at hand a leopard screamed. The jungle was beginning its regular nightly routine of kill or be killed.

Chapter 3   A Runaway Steam Roller!

A brief silence set in. And it was Chetah that broke it.

She had been hanging back, listening to the talk; Chetah was rather timid about strangers. But she had sidled up to Diana, and now plucked at her skirt. It was a gesture of friendliness.

Diana screamed and slapped at her. "Make this monkey stay away from me!" she cried out.

"Chetah, come here," Tarzan ordered. And, "She is not a monkey, but a chimpanzee. There is a greater gap in intelligence between a monkey and Chetah than there is between Chetah and us humans."

"I don't care what kind of creature she is," Diana said crossly. Then, "Are we just going to stand here and talk?"

"No." Tarzan turned away. "Follow me, all of you— single file."

The rocky ledge, which was about three feet wide, was very fortunately situated for his purpose. Striding along it, he moved about a hundred yards away from the place where the plane had gone into the canyon, with the others straggling along behind him.

They began talking. Diana said, "Camage, stop treading on my heels!" And, "I want to know where we're going!"

Dick Penrod said, "Diana, we have to trust him, do what he says. If he doesn't help us, nobody else will."

"Can't see any sense in walking on these rocks," Hal Fletcher grumbled. "Why don't we go down?"

Tarzan glanced around. "Stay on this ledge!"

He did not mean to leave any tracks for the Oparians.

Hawkins, he had noted, was bringing up the rear, moving reluctantly but still following along.

Presently Tarzan leaped from the ledge to a boulder, from that to another massive rock jutting out of the ground. He crossed a stretch of gray slate that would also show no footprints, and reached the jungle.

Tarzan plunged into it. Twilight shadows were already thick here. The others stumbled after him through the heavily matted undergrowth, fighting off the long trailing vines, exclaiming as thorns ripped their clothing. Tarzan looked back and said, "Quiet!"

They continued to grumble though, as time passed and he kept going. Hal Fletcher spoke querulously. "I can't take any more of this!"

Tarzan ignored him. He was keeping one eye on the sky, watching sunlight fade there. Tarzan knew of no tribe in Africa whose members moved about in the jungle after dark. They feared the evil spirits that were supposed to appear only at night. There was another reason, also, that kept them close to their fires: most of the predatory beasts did their hunting during the dark hours.

He came suddenly to a wide break in the jungle, an open area extending off to southward. Such breaks were fairly common in jungle of this type, which gradually merged with the Sahara on the north and the veldt, or open African plain, on the south. In the great Congo rain forest, westward, there would be no breaks at all.

Tarzan went on across the open space and again into the jungle on its far side. A little farther along he stopped.

The others came slowly along, to stop and group about him. With the exception of Hawkins, they were all badly worn. Studying them, Tarzan wondered how they could ever survive the hard trek back to civilization, if only an hour or so of not-too-difficult jungle travel could do this to them. But the effort to get them back had to be made.

He said, "We'll night here. Does any of you have a means of making fire?"

Tarzan could kindle flame himself, any one of several different ways, but it would take time to do so.

Hal Fletcher sulkily shook his head. Hawkins took off his hat and inspected its inner band. "Usually carry some matches here, but don't see any now."

Dick Penrod produced a gold cigarette lighter.

Chetah had aloofly ignored all of them since being rebuffed by Diana. She had stayed close to Tarzan, occasionally swinging into the trees, begging him to leave these people and join her there. But now, as the lighter glittered in the late sun, she could not resist the curiosity that impelled her to sidle up to Dick for a closer look—just as he thumbed it.

As it spurted fire, Chetah yelped in fright and did a complete back flip, then hurtled frenziedly around in a circle. She bumped into Camage Dean, who cried out and sat down hard. Chetah next ran up Hal Fletcher's back. Fletcher shouted angrily, flailing his arms. He lost his

balance and went headfirst into a bank of wet leaf-mold.

Chetah had leaped from Fletcher's back to a liana. She swung back and forth on that, grinding her teeth together, lips skinned back, screaming her opinion of these whites and of Tarzan's foolishness in having anything to do with them. Fire she understood, and quite well—but not fire that seemed to come from a man's thumb.

Tarzan's lips twitched in a smile. Then Fletcher scrambled up. The whole front of him, including his face and hair, was plastered with wet green leaf-mold. He glared around, snatched up a stick, and started toward Chetah with it raised to strike.

Tarzan moved quickly. He plucked the stick from Hal Fletcher's hand and tossed it aside. "Enough of that! You aren't hurt."

"No smart ape is going to make a fool out of me!" Fletcher raged. "You run that bundle of moth-eaten fur away from here or—or—"

Then his voice died, before Tarzan's cold gaze. He turned aside and sat down, chin sullenly on his chest.

Dick Penrod said, "It was my fault. I'm sorry. Is there any way I can convince your pet that I didn't mean to frighten her, Tarzan?"

"She isn't my pet," Tarzan answered. "Chetah is free to come and go as she pleases—but she is one of this party, and will not leave unless she wishes to do so. There'll be no more talk about driving her away. As for her fright, she'll soon get over it."

"All this concern about that—that creature!" Diana said petulantly. "Why doesn't somebody do some worrying about me? I'm tired and hungry!"

"You and Miss Dean, sit down and rest," Tarzan told her. "Penrod, you and Fletcher gather some dry wood and start a fire, a small one. Let it burn down to hot coals."

"Yeah?" Hal Fletcher said sulkily. "And just what are you going to be doing while we work?"

"I'll find food for your supper. All of you, stay right here while I'm gone. Don't wander away!" Then, "Hawkins, how many cartridges do you have for that rifle?"

The lanky man squinted slyly at him. "Enough."

"Keep watch with it then."

Hawkins said, "Been wondering about all this caution. We could have stopped just as easy by the canyon. Why did we have to come here?"

"Keep a sharp watch," Tarzan repeated. He felt the possibility of attack by the Oparians had passed, and could see no reason why he should confide in Hawkins.

A gesture then to Chetah, indicating that she should stay here, with Chetah grimacing angrily when she saw it; then Tarzan was gone, fading quickly into the jungle, going into the trees as soon as he was beyond sight of camp.

He climbed quickly to the upper reaches, pausing there to study a darkening sky, the flights of birds, nostrils testing the night wind, listening hard. All of his senses together told him what he wanted to know, and he started moving again. Presently he came to a jungle water hole.

These widely scattered spots, where springs bubbled or rain collected in hollows, were the twilight meeting places of all the jungle's creatures. Here a strange truce existed during the brief period between sunset and full night. Water was vital for life, and even the great killer beasts granted their usual prey the right to drink.

Perched on a limb near the water hole, Tarzan settled into absolute immobility as he studied the scene there.

Lions came at a sedate pace to dip their muzzles, then to yawn and shake themselves and daintily preen their whiskers. Zebra in their striped convict-suits kicked and brayed and frolicked briefly. Hartebeest, waterbuck, impala, and gnu, all of the antelope family, appeared out of the dusk to slake their thirst and fade swiftly away again.

Wart hogs grunted and squealed, clashing tusks with their cousins, the giant forest hogs. Gray jackals and spotted hyenas slunk furtively to the muddy margin of the water hole, growled at by the lions but not molested, providing they did not linger.

It was a busy, fascinating sight. Birds were also present— storks, cranes, and herons, stalking through the shallows on their stiltlike legs. There were hooting eagle owls, giant woodpeckers, bulbuls—birds of brilliant plumage and also the small drab birds that were always found near rhino, which might indicate that rhino were somewhere near.

A black leopard appeared from nowhere, snarling, drinking briefly, vanishing. Buffalo wallowed and grunted at the upper end of the pool, big sullen creatures with wide, curving horns. Numbers of eland and red bush duiker—more of the antelopes—appeared and left.

Suddenly all were silent, and the lions took themselves off. Only one creature could make Numa behave in such a fashion. Out of the forest, moving as quietly as shadows, came half a dozen elephants, great ears—like ragged palm-leaves—gently waving, trunks lifted to test the air, then dipping to suck up water. They were murmuring, a quiet sort of talk at twilight, and leisurely hosing each other down, since their wrinkled-looking hides, which looked so thick and tough, were actually quite sensitive and required frequent moistening.

It was very still about the pool until the elephants moved away again. Tantor, with his great bulk, keen intelligence, and ferocious power when enraged, was the lord of all jungle animals.

Tarzan suddenly stirred. The scene below was one that never failed to interest him, but he had not been watching it only for entertainment. He had been waiting. And now the object of his wait appeared—dik-dik, a small herd of them warily approaching.

They were pygmy antelopes, standing hardly more than a foot high. Tarzan let them drink, while singling out a fat young buck. Then he dropped among them, and as the others fled for cover he twisted the buck's neck quickly, mercifully.

It cleared all of the other creatures but the buffalo away from the pool. Tarzan knelt and drank sparingly himself, then dressed the antelope out, slung it over a shoulder, leaped to the trees and started back. He could as easily have chosen an eland or an impala, but there was no need.

He had more than sufficient meat for all, this night.

Tarzan worked toward that open break through the jungle, dropped down there, and went on afoot. The dik-dik was not heavy, but it did hamper him in the trees.

He was trotting easily along, almost back to the place which he had chosen for the night's camp, when scent and hearing warned of someone ahead of him in the open. A mingling of odors, perfume and powder among them, told him who it was—one of those two white women. His order that no one should leave the camp had been disobeyed.

The deep jungle night was over the land now, with a dusting of stars and some light from a rising moon—enough light for Tarzan to make out the woman, a moving blob of white ahead of him.

Then she screamed, a high-pitched, hysterical sound, and Tarzan recognized the voice of Diana Penrod. Beyond her suddenly appeared an eerie, phosphorescent glow, thin and wavering, outlining a ghostlike shape of something monstrously big. The thud of heavy hoofs pounded the earth. A deep-toned grunt sounded, then an angry, suspicious squeal. Those hoofs began to beat the ground like a kettle-drum; the wavering phosphorescent glow rushed at the helpless woman.

Tarzan dropped the dik-dik carcass and raced to her. She was trying to run, stumbling over the uneven ground as she attempted to get out of the way of the charging monster. Tarzan whipped an arm about her waist, threw her over his shoulder, and whirled toward the trees.

A thunder of sound pursued him. It was like being chased by a runaway steam roller, one that could twist and turn, following his every move.

The woman was screaming and clawing at him. Tarzan leaped high, gripped a branch, and pulled himself up. A second later, cyclonic violence hurtled against the tree he had chosen. It was big and deeply rooted, but it groaned and shook under that ferocious impact.

Tarzan and Diana were not in that tree, however. He had leaped quickly to another. "Take hold of the trunk there and hold on tight," he told her. And, tonelessly, "Perhaps you understand now why I told everyone to stay put."

"Wh-what is it?" she gasped. The other tree was being hit again. Monkeys were screaming in fear, rushing blindly in all directions through the dark about them. The whole jungle had come alive, with furious angry roarings at this interruption of the night quiet.

"That," Tarzan said, "is a rhino, and a big one."

"But—that glow! What makes it?"

"There are times when they glow like that at night. Nobody knows the reason. Perhaps it's something they eat. Stay here now. I'll be back in a couple of minutes—"

"You'll not leave me!" Diana cried. "I could never stand it!"

"You must. I have to send him away."

Diana said blankly, "Send him away? Why, you must be mad!"

"No. Just practical. That other tree will go over in a minute; he'll scent us here, and start butting this one. He has to be stopped, before he hurts or kills himself."

"Before what?" Diana said unbelievingly. "Get me away from here! I don't care what happens to a stupid, vicious beast!"

"Stupid, perhaps, but not vicious—only afraid of man, for good reason. And I care," Tarzan said quietly. "There are too few of his kind left in Africa . . . ."

Tarzan dropped to the ground and walked forward, toward the great engine of destruction that had just rammed that other tree, the object of its wrath, a third time. The tree was still standing, though it leaned now at an acute angle.

The rhino scented and turned toward Tarzan. It pawed the ground, warning with an enraged grunt that in another second it would charge him.

Tarzan moved lightly, balanced on the balls of his feet. There was more moonlight now, which was helpful but not much needed; Tarzan had superlative night vision.

The rhino was an enormous specimen, with the single curving horn of its kind thrusting up from its snout. Its head lowered. It pawed the ground again.

"Ka-goda!" Tarzan said. *"Ib-harrugh!"* He was speaking in the deep, throaty grunts of the great apes, the first vocal speech he had ever known, reverting to the days of his youth.

The rhino squealed. It backed off a step, some bewilderment in its small dim brain. Scent told it this creature was human and white, and so hateful, but unhuman sounds were reaching its ears.

"The jungle is our mother," Tarzan said. "I speak its truce between us—"

The rhino squealed again, and came at him in a whirlwind rush of fury. Its great bulk touched Tarzan's body. The murderous horn hooked up at him like the slash of a saber, seeking to rip him open.

Chapter 4   Night in the Jungle

Tarzan stood his ground until the rough hide brushed against his skin. Then he slid swiftly aside, one step only. The rhino rushed on past. It had dim eyesight, relying on scent and sound for guidance, and charged in a straight line, so that evasion was not difficult—if one had cold nerve, waited until the last split-second, and then leaped away very quickly.

The horn grazed Tarzan slightly. The rhino charged furiously on into the trees, thrashed about, squealing continually, finally came to a baffled halt, wheeled around, and returned to the open again.

"Ka-gunda!" Tarzan said. "We belong to the jungle. I am not your enemy, mighty one."

He walked slowly forward then. There was a feeling of sadness in Tarzan. This great beast, armored like a tank,

so menacing that even the most evil-tempered bull elephant left him strictly alone, actually had been stranded
by Nature in a time where it did not belong. The rhinoceros had no natural enemy save one—man. And because
it did not have the intelligence to cope with man, it was
swiftly vanishing.

Tarzan walked up to the hulking brute. It was breathing
hard, panting sounds like the exhaust of a steam engine.
Tarzan reached out and scratched gently between its eyes.
Its horn rubbed against his arm. Actually, it was not horn
at all, but a solidified growth of hair as hard as any tusk
of ivory.

"Friend, go in peace," Tarzan grunted.

The rhino snorted, backed off several steps—and abruptly
trotted away, perhaps puzzling over this strange human
who did not seem human at all, though it was more likely
that within five minutes the animal had no memory whatever of the occurrence.

Tarzan went to recover the dik-dik carcass, leaped to
the trees again, and reached the one where Diana waited.

"You were crazy to take such a risk as that, completely
crazy!" she said. Then, "What are you doing? Stop! Put
me down!"

He had unceremoniously lifted her. The dik-dik was over one shoulder, and Diana was now slung over the other. Tarzan had carried heavier burdens. With both hands free he swung swiftly through the branches, the woman crying out in protest and hammering his back with her fists. A few fleeting moments later he dropped into the camp.

Tarzan tried to ease the woman down then, but she squirmed away from him, flailing with both arms so violently that she fell to the ground and rolled ungracefully there, still making angry sounds.

A small fire was burning as Tarzan had ordered, with a bed of coals waiting. He saw Camage Dean staring at him fearfully. She had screamed with fright as he came leaping down out of the night.

Hal Fletcher, standing by the fire, had started violently also. He now stared at the dik-dik. "Is that all you brought back with you?" Fletcher demanded.

"Did you expect me to return with a six-course dinner, including demitasse and dessert?" Tarzan inquired coldly. Then he turned to Hawkins, standing nearby with rifle over his arm. "Where is Dick Penrod?"

Hawkins shrugged. "Tore out of here to look for his wife. She slipped away, but we didn't notice that until we heard a racket. I told him it was a rhino, likely had treed the woman if it hadn't trampled her, and either way there wasn't anything we could do, but he went to hunt for her anyway."

Tarzan sighed inwardly. Now he would have to go and search for Penrod. But a moment later Dick came struggling into the circle of firelight.

"I saw you rushing through the trees, heard Diana and knew from the tone of her voice that she was all right," he told Tarzan. Then he turned to his wife. "Diana, why did you go away like that?"

Diana had scrambled to her feet. She tossed her head angrily. "I did it to show him that nobody gives me orders! And that—that savage mauled me around like I was a sack of potatoes! He risked breaking my neck by hauling me through the trees—"

"Outrageous!" Hal Fletcher snapped. He glared at Tarzan. "I think you did it only to impress us with the way you can swing from branches. Well, any monkey can do it better!"

Diana nodded approvingly. "There was no need for it, no need at all! There was that open space in the jungle. We could have walked back!"

Tarzan, kneeling, was slicing steaks from the dik-dik haunch. "You seldom find one rhino alone. The mate of the one that charged you was likely nearby, in the open space you're talking about. They don't like thick jungle, and probably wandered in here from the veldt somewhere to the south. I didn't want to run the risk of facing another of them in the dark; that's why I came back through the trees."

Diana sniffed and tossed her head again. "You needn't have been so rough about it! And you needn't have been in such a hurry, either, to get back here!"

Tarzan did not comment on this. But the thought of prowling leopards had hurried him on that return. Now he rose, looked around, found a number of short sticks, drove them into the ground by the bed of coals, and impaled the steaks on them.

"These should be ready soon," he said. "Each of you select one, watch it for the degree you wish it to be cooked, and then eat."

He withdrew from the fire to eat his own meal. Cooked foods did not have much flavor for Tarzan; now, as customarily, he ate his meat raw, realizing the others were watching him and that this act probably increased their opinion of his savagery, though Fletcher presently snatched up a steak and gnawed on it hungrily though the meat was scarcely seared.

Diana had had some angry words for Dick Penrod, not bothering to lower her voice: "As usual, you stand around without a word to say! That—that person treated me outrageously; you should give him a good dressing-down!"

"But, Diana, Tarzan knows this country and its dangers. I think he was right when he told us all to stay here—"

She turned her back on him and walked around the fire to sit beside Hal Fletcher. Some of their words reached Tarzan.

"He's obviously only a muscle-bound oaf," Fletcher said. "More savage than any native and no wonder, from what Hawkins told us about him being raised by apes in the jungle and all the rest of it. But don't worry, Diana, when the right time comes I'll tell him off!"

And from Diana, "He and that rhinoceros talked to each other! The most hideous sounds imaginable! And the monster trotted away when he told it to!"

Tarzan had to smile. No one had ever talked with a rhinoceros, any more than with a giraffe, which could make no sounds at all. He had hoped only to lull the rhino with words that might stir some dim feeling in the animal's dull brain that the manlike thing facing it was friendly. The try had worked. Another time it might not.

Deep night was over the jungle now, with the moon obscured by drifting clouds. It was strangely quiet, because man was abroad in the jungle. Tarzan thought worriedly of those Oparian warriors who could not be very far away.

Chetah came sliding down a liana. She had been foraging for her own supper among the trees; no one ever had to find food for her.

Camage Dean, kneeling beside the fire and watching the steaks, lifted one. She meant to eat the steak herself, but Diana spoke imperiously: "That one looks fairly well done, Camage. Bring it to me."

The plump woman meekly obeyed, then returned to start watching another steak.

Tarzan studied all of them thoughtfully. Camage Dean had been termed a companion of Diana Penrod, but she seemed to be actually a sort of browbeaten servant. Hal Fletcher was a blustering loud-mouth, and Tarzan wondered how he had happened to be along on that ill-fated plane trip.

Hawkins needed no thought or appraisal. The one-time white hunter was sitting back from the fire, rifle across his knees. He would not give a snap of his fingers to save anyone here; that Josiah Hawkins made out all right was his only concern.

The thing that Tarzan wondered about most was the scolding, ill-tempered attitude of Diana toward Dick Penrod, and the silent, weary way Dick accepted it.

There should be some good in the woman, Tarzan thought, remembering her fearful manner when she had realized Dick was still in the plane, there at the edge of the canyon. But that had been only momentary. She was willful, selfish; she had caused trouble already and would probably cause more.

As for Dick, there seemed to be good stuff in him, also, though it must be buried deep. Tarzan hoped it could be brought out. He was going to need help from someone here, if these people were to escape from the jungle.

Chetah plucked at his arm, begging again that they leave, and let the others work out their own problems.

"No," Tarzan murmured. "They'd never make it alone, Chetah. We have to stay with them, even though they may not appreciate it and forget to thank us at the end."

Chetah snorted, grimacing at this, and chattered her opinion that Tarzan was being very foolish. Then she selected a liana, climbed up it twenty feet or so, and went to sleep. She did not like to sleep on the ground or in the trees; leopards prowled there. Huddled like a ball of fur on a trailing vine, she was safe from about anything with the exception of her mortal enemy, the baboon. But this was not baboon country.

They were all huddled about the fire, sleeping uneasily, with the exception of Hawkins who was dozing in a sitting position. Tarzan dropped silently from the trees and added several sticks to the fire.

He had been out for a wary look around, testing the night air with his nostrils, analyzing each sound that came to him. Somewhere nearby a leopard was coughing, but it had already fed and was heading toward its lair. A jackal yapped briefly, and a lion roared a warning for it to be off.

The night was still very quiet. Standing by the fire, looking at those asleep, Tarzan hoped it would stay this way.

They had turned in early. Fletcher had growled a surly request: "How about bringing us some water to drink? I'm dry as a bone."

"Sorry," Tarzan had told him. "That'll have to wait until morning." And he would have to find something better for them to drink than the muddy fluid in the water hole.

"You mean to say that there's something you can't do?" Fletcher had said sneeringly.

Now, at this late hour with all of them asleep, the night stillness was suddenly broken by a distant thudding sound, far off—the beating of a drum.

Or—probably not a drum. It was more likely someone thumping a hollow log with two sticks. But it produced a sound that carried far, which was the intent of the man making it. Only a few swift beats with silence following, a questioning call that was answered by a similar sound nearer at hand, no more than a couple of miles away, if that much.

Then the two drums were talking. Tarzan listened intently.

He had known drum talk as long as he could remember. Throughout the length and breadth of equatorial Africa the drums were always beating. And a simple code governed nearly all of them, expressive of ideas and symbols rather than words.

The reason for that uniform drum code was the hundreds and hundreds of different languages spoken in Africa, so many of them that frequently the natives of villages no more than two or three miles apart spoke tongues that were completely strange to each other and could communicate only on the drums.

The code being used tonight was a little different, a little more complicated, but after a couple of minutes Tarzan was able to read it with no trouble.

The drum-beater close at hand belonged to the Oparians he had encountered on the game trail; after reporting the whereabouts of those warriors, the signaler added that a white man had been seen by them, an extraordinary white man who ran with swiftness and ease through the tops of trees, escaping.

They had split up and had searched through the jungle for the white man without success. While separated, they had seen a great metal bird, trailing smoke, fly over the jungle and crash with a thunderous sound. It had been too late in the day to search for the metal bird and learn whether any who had been in it were still alive. The ten in that party had made a night camp, where they were at the present time.

Tarzan now realized that there were two groups of Oparians. The second party must be eighteen or twenty miles away. He wondered how many were in it. And some important chief, who was with the second, distant party, was the leader of both groups, for now the distant drum beats began to issue orders.

The search was to be resumed at dawn for the white man who had escaped. Half of the ten were to take up that hunt. The other half were to search for and find the metal bird, taking captive any who might have survived the crash. And that distant group would move east to join forces with the group of ten.

The final part of the message thudded through the night: "The time of the blood moon is near again. We must have whites for the sacrifices. Do not forget—five is the number. Do not fail!"

Then a double-roll on both drums indicated that the talk was over.

Not until then did Tarzan discover that someone else here had been listening to it. A sudden brief glitter, from firelight shining against opened eyes, told him Josiah Hawkins was awake. The lanky man had spent many years in the jungle and on the veldt; he could not have failed to learn drum talk and to have read the messages passing back and forth this night.

Hawkins quickly closed his eyes again, perhaps aware of Tarzan's frowning scrutiny. But a strange sort of mocking smile showed on his face.

Tarzan moved back into darkness, well away from the fire, and sat down cross-legged to think about it—those messages and Hawkins' reaction to them.

He thought again of what he had learned from the young district commissioner who had started him on this hunt. Five white men had disappeared in this area—one missionary, two oil explorers, and two men who had been hunting alone in the hope of capturing a live bongo—the fabled blue antelope which it was said might not even exist, since no white man had ever seen one. They were wrong in that; Tarzan had seen bongo a number of times.

Was there something significant in the number five? It had been mentioned in the drum talk. Five white men had disappeared. Perhaps it was a sacred number in the savage Oparian religion, as seven was a sacred number in many native African cults.

And there was that mention also of a blood moon, whose time was near. This would seem to indicate the Oparians sacrificed to their gods once a year, with five white victims needed. Tarzan glanced at those sleeping about the fire. There were six whites here, more than enough for the sacrificial rites—or five, if Josiah Hawkins was not counted.

Hawkins had been to Opar. He had heard the drum talk and did not seem worried. Hawkins, Tarzan told himself, might have been guiding that plane to Opar on a much more sinister errand than any effort to trade for ivory. He must be watched very carefully.

One thing was certain. A sizable number of Oparian warriors had left their mountain country to search across the plains and through the jungle for whites. They had succeeded hereabouts in snaring those they needed at the last blood moon, and were hunting in the same area again.

Unless Tarzan moved fast, they might succeed again.

With this final thought he settled himself to get some rest before dawn—still sitting as he was, eyes not quite closed, a wakeful sort of dozing. It was the sleep of the wild. One part of Tarzan's brain relaxed while another part took over, automatically noting every sound in the night, every shift of air currents and the scents they brought, but blocking off all that did not warn of danger.

The night slowly waned. The moon, which was in its

first quarter, set at about three, and it became very dark. Sometime later Chetah suddenly stirred, with a drowsy mutter of warning.

"I hear it," Tarzan murmured. "Sleep, little one."

Chetah sighed and was silent. A soft rustling came from the thick jungle tangles nearby, and an almost inaudible growl.

Many animals had been drawn by curiosity to investigate the fire, to back off quickly when they detected the scent of man. But this one lingered, growling again.

Tarzan knew what it was—a leopard. His first thought had been that it was the same one he had heard before, which had fed. But suddenly he knew it was not, and rose to his feet, unsheathing his knife.

This was a precautionary move only; it was never wise to ignore any possibility where a leopard was concerned.

Hawkins had come awake, also. Tarzan saw his rifle shift in the direction of that growl, which had the sound of a distant buzz saw.

No one could predict what a leopard might do. It could be driven by hunger to attack anything, even man, and would also kill without reason for the sheer savage love of killing.

The timbre of its growl told Tarzan that this one had found the hunting poor tonight; it had eaten, but not very well. Perhaps it had been drawn by the blood smell of the dik-dik carcass, and would ignore the menacing scent of humans in an attempt to get at it.

Chetah suddenly scrambled a dozen feet higher on the liana; leopards could leap for incredible distances, and were fond of chimpanzee flesh.

An instant later, soundlessly, the leopard was beside the fire, crouched low, virtually invisible. But its eyes were sparks of greenish fire. Tarzan glanced at Hawkins, who did not move. Tarzan started toward the animal.

And Camage Dean stirred and sighed, rising sleepily, looking around. She said dazedly, "Where am I? What—"

The leopard screamed, an unearthly sound it uttered to freeze its prey in panicky fear, and leaped at her, a streak of motion almost too fast for any human eye to follow.

But Tarzan had moved faster, hurdling the fire, throwing himself between the cat and the woman.

The leopard struck him with violence—ripping claws and slashing, razor-sharp teeth. It was still screaming. Tarzan went down with the animal on top of him.

Chapter 5   Back to the Plane

Tarzan was not driven flat by the leopard's impact. He fell backward by deliberate design, pulling the animal down with him.

There were a number of ways of defending one's self against the charge of this great jungle cat, but meeting it head on, while standing erect, was not one of them. A leopard always fought the same way, slashing with teeth and foreclaws at the throat, while raking with hind claws at the middle, an effort to rip its adversary open.

Thus it was to evade both murderous moves that Tarzan threw himself backward and down, twisting so he landed on his side, knees drawn up to protect his mid-section. As he fell, he sought and gained a hold of his own, the steely grip of his left hand at the back of the leopard's neck.

No animal in Africa was more powerful, pound for

pound, than this killer cat. Still screaming, legs churning as it attempted to use its hooked claws, teeth snapping with a sound like many knives pressed against whirling grindstones, it fought with full unleashed fury to rip Tarzan's flesh.

Still maintaining the grip against its neck, he whipped the leopard on its side so that he was behind the animal. His right arm flashed up and down in two lightning-swift strokes, driving his knife deep; then he let the leopard go, leaping back and away, crouching, ready to move in again.

It was not necessary. His knife had found the leopard's savage heart.

And he turned suddenly on Hawkins. "Take your finger off that trigger!"

Hawkins had his rifle raised to fire. "Might as well use a bullet and make sure of the critter," he protested.

Tarzan shook his head. "Don't do any shooting at any time, unless I tell you to." The sound of a rifle shot would instantly alert the Oparians and mark the position of this camp.

"Yeah?" Hawkins said challengingly. "And just why not?"

The leopard's scream had awakened the others here.

They were milling confusedly about. Camage Dean still stood where she had been when the leopard leaped at her. One of its paws was over her foot. Tarzan moved to her with quick concern. "You're all right?"

"Why, yes," she answered, sounding surprised. "I suppose I should be nearly scared to death—but I'm not. It's a very strange feeling . . . You're hurt!"

"It's nothing." There were some scratches on his chest and right arm; it was too much to hope that any person could fight a leopard at such close quarters and emerge entirely unmarked.

Chetah came sliding down the liana to do a triumphant dance around the leopard. She snatched a tuft of black fur and paraded about, waving it over her head.

Hal Fletcher spoke fretfully to Tarzan: "That beast might have killed all of us where we slept. Why didn't you go and drive it away before it could get that close?"

"If I had tried to drive away every animal that has come to take a look at us, I'd have had no time for rest myself," Tarzan answered. "They have been prowling close all night—at least one other leopard, three or four lions at different times, jackals and hyenas. They were only curious. This one was hungry."

He knelt, put wood on the fire, and by its light began to skin out the leopard's hide. Camage had gone away; now she returned with a strip of cloth torn from her underskirt, and insisted on dabbing at his scratches with it.

Then Diana spoke to her: "My back is as stiff as a board from sleeping on that hard ground. Camage, come here and rub it."

Camage hesitated. Diana snapped, "Do as I say!"

Camage obeyed her.

Tarzan quickly finished the work of removing the leopard's hide. Hal Fletcher said, "What are you going to do with that? If there's one thing we don't need, it's a heavy hide to have to pack around!"

Tarzan rolled up the hide, then took the leopard carcass some distance into the jungle. He dropped it and started back. Before he had gone a dozen paces a medley of barks, yaps, and snarls began—hyenas and jackals, the scavengers of the jungle, fighting over that carcass.

The night was beginning to break. Tarzan searched among the trees, seeking a certain type of supple vine and cutting down various lengths. Chetah, who had accompanied him, helped Tarzan haul them back to the fire. She knew why he wanted those vines.

At the camp Tarzan settled himself again in a cross-legged position and set to work, splitting a hard outer covering on the vines, peeling it away to reveal a tough green core.

The others watched him work. It was Dick Penrod who cleared his throat and asked, "What are you doing?"

"Getting ready to go down to the wreckage of your plane, as soon as it is light, and salvage what I can of your supplies," Tarzan replied.

"But you said nobody could get down there!" Dick protested.

"No. What I said was that nobody in your party could do it," Tarzan told him.

They were back at the canyon with the first gray light of dawn. Tarzan had scouted carefully for some sign of the Oparians. There was none.

It was quite cold in these moments just before sunrise. Diana said, "Why can't we make a fire?"

The reason was that Tarzan wanted no telltale smoke by daylight to guide the Oparians here, but he could not say so. He did not want to panic these people.

En route to the canyon, Dick Penrod had told of the

supplies carried in the plane. "Some food and water stored aft of the cabin—but not very much of either—along with our luggage and the stuff we meant to trade at Opar for ivory. We didn't even think about being forced down, and brought along the water and some cans of food only in case we couldn't acquire what we might need either at that town in the Sudan or at Opar."

"What about firearms and cartridges?" Tarzan asked.

Dick shook his head. "None of either. The authorities at Nairobi won't allow guns or shells to be carried in a plane, for fear they might fall into the hands of the Mau Mau killers, unless a licensed white hunter is aboard. And Hawkins isn't licensed. He got that rifle of his into the ship somehow, said he never went anywhere without it, and hang the authorities."

So the only firearm in the party was in the possession of a man whom Tarzan thoroughly distrusted.

Tarzan and Penrod were walking ahead of the others as they approached the canyon. Tarzan had a coil of improvised rope over his shoulder, a hundred-odd feet of the vines he had cored out, tied together. He carried the leopard hide under his arm.

Chetah had dashed on to the canyon rim. There she

threw rocks down at the smashed plane, and called to Tarzan to hurry.

Tarzan spoke bluntly, "Penrod, I think you have a fair amount of common sense. Didn't it strike you as a pretty risky and foolish thing to do, flying into wild and uncharted country to trade for ivory that may not even exist, with nothing to go on but the word of a man like Josiah Hawkins?"

Dick chewed his lip. He said presently, "Diana had a sudden whim in New York, two months back, to go on a big-game safari, encouraged by Fletcher, who came along. Camage came because she has been a sort of companion to Diana for years. It all cost a lot of money, which didn't matter to Diana. She let Fletcher handle the bills, and he's been taking a fat percentage for himself—but Diana wouldn't listen when I tried to tell her that."

From the tone of Dick Penrod's voice, Diana often had expensive whims, and there was probably someone like Fletcher always around to profit from them.

"We took a big safari out of Nairobi: ten trucks, four white hunters, and a hundred natives," Dick went on. "Within a week we were back. Safari life bored Diana. She wanted to do something novel and different. Then Fletcher came up with Hawkins and that scheme of his to fly to Opar."

They had reached the canyon. Tarzan moved along it until he found a jutting boulder that was firmly set in the ground. He tied one end of his vine-rope about the boulder, pulling hard to make sure it would hold.

"Sure, it sounded weird to me," Penrod continued. "But Diana had already bought the plane and made all arrangements before I even knew about it. According to the flight clearance, we were supposed to be going to Tanganyika to photograph elephants. It was too late for me to stop her. Diana said I could come along and pilot the plane—I had seven years of flying with the U.S. Navy—or she would hire a pilot and I could go on back to New York. I—I couldn't let her fly off like that; I came along, hoping for the best."

Tarzan dropped his rope into the canyon. It reached within several feet of the bottom.

He had a clear picture now of Diana—spoiled, selfish, determined to have her own way in everything.

And what of Dick Penrod? No man who had flown for the U. S. Navy could be a coward. Dick had a backbone then. Perhaps, Tarzan thought, he had just never found a way to say No to Diana and make it stick.

The others came straggling along now, Diana complaining about the cold.

Tarzan faced them. "It is time to tell you what we must do when I return from the canyon. I will guide you back to civilization." He would have to postpone his search for Opar, but that could not be helped.

He knelt in the dirt and began to draw a map with his finger. "This is the coastline of the Indian Ocean. And here—" he drew an X some inches to the left of it "—is about where we are now. This—" his finger moved somewhat to the right, drawing a crooked line "—is the Ngamu River. Steamboats go up almost to its headwaters. The Ngamu is south and east of us—about five days' journey, I think, though I have never been through the country between here and the river. It will undoubtedly be very hard going, but I will do my best to get you to the Ngamu."

He stood up again. They were all silent for a moment. Then Diana said, "Hawkins, is he telling the truth?"

Tarzan felt a surge of anger, but kept it firmly in check. He was interested in Hawkins' reply.

The lanky man nodded promptly. "Yeah. The Ngamu is there, like he says. About as good a way as any there is to get out of this fix, I suppose."

Tarzan now felt mild surprise. He had expected Hawkins to give a different sort of answer, perhaps claim that they could still make it on to Opar.

Diana spoke again, to Tarzan: "There's only one thing you haven't said—how much you want to be paid for guiding us. Well, I'll be generous, but I don't intend to be held up!"

"There'll be no charge at all," Tarzan told her coldly, and left them, going to the canyon rim.

Dick went with him. He muttered, "She's upset and tired, and also frightened. Please don't take offense!"

"I shan't," Tarzan said. "And I'll go down now. You watch the rope for me. Don't let anyone touch it. Keep everybody back. I'll return as quickly as possible."

He caught hold and went over the rim, walking quickly down, feet against the rock wall. Chetah came after him, hand over hand. She jumped when still a dozen feet above the canyon bed and scampered ahead to the wreckage of the plane.

It took only a glance for Tarzan to realize he could not hope to find much here that might be useful. The torn-away tail section had been broken, twisted, and crumpled, with its contents all mixed up in ruined metal. Only an acetylene torch could separate them.

But some things had been thrown clear. Tarzan picked up a number of tins: some, processed beef, others, English biscuits. He also found a gallon metal flask, still full of water, and then a bolt of red cotton cloth—trade goods.

The plane's fuselage was upright. Tarzan went into the cabin through the still-opened door. The furniture had been ripped loose and smashed to tangles of wood and leather. But the green velvet drapes were still looped back at the plane's windows; he took all of them. In the pilot's cubicle he discovered another metal flask, this one empty, and then a real find: a cardboard box containing ten chocolate bars.

Chetah meanwhile had been investigating also, and had made a collection of her own, objects of fascination to a chimpanzee with a taste for anything bright and shiny. She had acquired a smashed chronometer, a blue doorknob, a piece of broken mirror, a long steel rod, and a heavy brass ring as big as a bracelet. This made an armful for her, and she started to lug it out of the plane, grunting in satisfaction.

Tarzan said, "We can't take that stuff with us. You'd soon get tired and want me to carry it for you. And I'll have other things to do. Leave it here, Chetah."

She squealed in protest, hugging her treasures.

"No," Tarzan said. "Put it down!"

Chetah began a speech the meaning of which was plain. She had to have these items. They would make her friends, the chimps along the Ruwenzori, green with envy when at last she and Tarzan returned home.

"You can keep that doorknob, or the brass ring—nothing else," Tarzan said. "The rest stays here!"

Chetah threw her armful on the floor and went to sit in a corner, where she made angry faces while muttering threats that she would go home alone, right now, today.

"You would run into baboons," Tarzan said. "Have you forgotten them? They would chase you and bite pieces out of you."

Chetah whimpered and tried to hide in the corner. She had indeed forgotten the baboons, those dog-faced creatures who delighted in tormenting chimpanzees.

Tarzan kept poking about in the wreckage. He found a suede jacket which must belong to Dick Penrod, and then a woman's cloth coat. Then he discovered a leather strap-bag with metal initials which indicated it was Camage Dean's property.

With this assortment, Tarzan told himself, he had to be content. He could spend no more time here.

"Carry some of these things," Tarzan said, handing the jacket and woman's bag to Chetah. She snorted her opinion of anyone who would take such trash and leave her treasures behind, then left the plane ahead of him.

Outside, Tarzan rolled everything together and put it in the coat, then buttoned that up, tied its sleeves together and made a sling that he hung around his neck. "Let's go," he told Chetah, and started back toward the dangling rope. It was just sunup, with the sky rose and pink overhead.

Chetah suddenly cried out, dropped the jacket and bag, and ran back into the plane. She emerged again, carefully gripping the heavy metal ring. She had not forgotten Tarzan's promise that this could be taken along.

At the rope, she leaped high, holding her things in one hand, climbing with both feet and her other hand. Tarzan gripped the rope and started to follow, walking up the sheer rock wall again. Halfway up, he noticed something overhead that abruptly doubled his speed.

It was a column of smoke climbing high in the sky.

He whipped himself over the canyon rim to see a fire crackling briskly nearby. Diana and Hal Fletcher stood with their hands outstretched to its warmth.

Tarzan turned to Dick Penrod. "Did you start that fire?" he demanded, voice tight and edged.

Dick shook his head. Josiah Hawkins spoke up from nearby. "It was me—found a match in my hatband after all. Couldn't see harm in a fire to warm us all up."

"Diana and I couldn't see any harm in it either," Hal Fletcher said. "Perhaps you don't mind being cold, Tarzan. We do."

But harm had been done. The telltale column of smoke must certainly have been seen by that near party of Oparians. They must have started toward it at once.

Tarzan put his bundle down. He brought out the flask of water and handed it to Penrod. "One drink apiece," he said. "Then we're leaving here. Get up on that rock ledge and lead out southward."

He bent to add the leopard hide to the other items wrapped up in the coat, then quickly retrieved his rope, coiling it.

"Why be in such a hurry?" Hawkins objected. "Here it's scarcely sunup, and we're all hungry. And there's a fire going; I can shoot something for breakfast. . . ."

The man's voice was suave, plausible-sounding. But his

eyes showed a hard glitter. Was he trying to hold them all
here for some dark purpose of his own, or was this only an
effort by Hawkins to push Tarzan aside and start giving
the orders?

"I'll handle the matter of food, as soon as I think it's safe
to stop," Tarzan said. "You'll save your cartridges, Hawkins, against the time when they may be badly needed.
You've had your drink. Get going!"

Hawkins had been standing with rifle partially raised,
pointing almost in Tarzan's direction. Now, with Tarzan's
eyes pin-pointing him, he hesitated a moment. About a
dozen feet separated them—not quite enough room for
Hawkins to swing his gun and fire before Tarzan could
cover that distance, if such a move was what Hawkins had
in mind. He made a sour face, the rifle slanting down, and
started off after Penrod.

The others straggled along the ledge, also. Tarzan took
the flask from Camage, who had used it last, returned it to
the bundle, picked that up, and followed them. Chetah,
he noticed, was trotting along beside Penrod, still carrying
the things she had brought out of the canyon. Tarzan saw
Dick Penrod reach down to take the chimp's hand.

About a half mile or so to southward, the jungle curved

in toward the canyon. If they could make it to that thick green cover before the Oparians came along, Tarzan thought, and gain a good lead, there would be a chance to elude the pursuing bronze warriors completely.

They did not quite make it. When they were still short of the jungle by a few hundred feet, an exultant, reverberating shout rang out behind them.

Tarzan whipped around to see one of the Oparians in the open, at the edge of the jungle where it ended near the spot the plane had gone into the canyon, shield lifted and spear pointing toward them.

Another of them came bursting into sight. This one carried a bow. He hastily notched an arrow and sent it high in whistling flight.

The distance was too long for effective shooting. The arrow, meant to scare rather than hurt, plunged down a good dozen yards short of Tarzan. The bowman ran toward them and paused to launch another shaft. Diana cried out in fright, a hysterical sound. The spearman shouted again: *"M-tu zanje! Molto!"* Many whites. It was a call to the others, still back in the jungle.

"Keep going!" Tarzan ordered. "Get in among the trees—hurry!"

Moments later the jungle had closed about them. They were safe—for the moment, anyway.

But those two scouting warriors would follow them, and the others would soon be along. Word would go to that second group of Oparians, somewhere off to westward, and they, too, would hurry to join the hunt.

It would be pressed hard. The Oparians had discovered that not one but six whites fled before them. Their search for victims to be sacrificed in the rites of the blood moon might be ended successfully before the just-risen sun had set tonight.

Chapter 6   The Deadly Race

They struggled along through tangled jungle depths, with the coolness of dawn now a distant memory. Heat was harsh and oppressive, increasing with each passing moment.

Tarzan worked constantly up and down the line, going ahead to find the easiest possible way through the dense undergrowth on the forest floor, then moving back to push all of them along.

For a time it was not necessary to do much urging. The appearance of those bronze warriors, and the flash of arrows in the sun, had frightened them—with the possible exception of Hawkins, who did not seem much perturbed.

Then, as time passed, the pace started to lag. Diana and Fletcher began to complain, voices rising in shrill protest; with covert prodding from Hawkins, Tarzan thought. He would hear the mutter of the man's voice, and then another complaint from those two.

There was reason enough for them to fret. The going was brutally hard, especially on the women, though Camage Dean was bearing up quietly. All of them were beginning to have blistered feet; their faces and arms were puffing, swelling, since every other plant in the jungle had some kind of thorn.

But Tarzan refused to allow a rest stop until four or five miles had been covered. Then he called a halt. All of them promptly slumped down. Diana said, "I can't go another step; I simply can't!"

Tarzan brought out the flask of water and allowed each another sparing drink. Fletcher tried to gulp more, and Tarzan had to snatch the flask from him. It was not a question of saving water. If the man drank any more, stomach cramps might result.

Hawkins said, "Seems to me this running is kind of unnecessary. Wouldn't have been any harm to get into the jungle and then stop; you and me could have gone back for a talk-talk with that pair. Only a couple of wandering hunters from some nearby tribe, likely, a mite overexcited at seeing whites in their country."

"Just what tribe would you say they're from, Hawkins?"

Tarzan asked. He studied the man closely.

"Why, probably Watusi."

"We're more than three hundred miles from Watusi country. Also, no Watusi ever had that bronze-colored skin; neither does any other native of any tribe you could name. None of them uses short horn bows; none would send an arrow at a white man."

"Could they be Mau Maus?" Dick Penrod asked.

"No. Mau Maus are all Kikuyus, and the nearest Kikuyu are farther away than the Watusi. What we saw were warriors from the north and east, out of the mountains of Ethiopia. There are a hundred wild tribes in those mountains who have never been conquered; they belong to one of them."

"Cannibals, maybe?" Penrod asked hesitantly.

"Maybe," Tarzan said. Let them think that; it should be enough to keep them moving.

He poured water into his cupped hand and offered it to Chetah. She drank gratefully. Chetah could swing tirelessly through the trees all day, but ground travel quickly wearied her.

"Little one, go back the way we came and see if anyone follows us," Tarzan said.

She nodded understandingly, leaped for a branch, and raced away. Tarzan then selected a towering tree and climbed to its top.

It was another of the hagenia species, the most common tree in the jungles of central Africa, something like a eucalyptus but with more branches and foliage. Now, from the lofty perch it afforded him, Tarzan devoted several minutes to a study of all the country about. Then he quickly descended.

"We're moving on," he announced. "Everybody up! Penrod, lead out—that way." He pointed eastward.

"I can't walk a step!" Diana cried.

Tarzan reached down and pulled the woman to her feet. "You must. Fletcher, get going."

Hal Fletcher glowered sourly, but struggled erect.

Hawkins muttered, "I still think you and me ought to go back for a talk-talk, Tarzan."

"I don't," Tarzan said. "Get started, Hawkins."

"Aren't you going to wait for Chetah?" Penrod asked.

"No. She'll find us." Tarzan added Chetah's bundle to his own. They started to move, a slow, shambling procession.

Chetah came along some minutes later, to drop to Tarzan's shoulder and chatter in his ear.

Penrod asked, "They're—following us?"

"Yes," Tarzan said. "Keep going."

It was later, with the morning now well along, when all of them suddenly exclaimed in relief; the jungle was beginning to thin out again, with open country visible off to southward. It was the edge of the veldt, the African plain.

Tarzan had known the veldt must be nearby, even before sighting it in his lofty survey. The presence of the rhino last night, the elephants, lions, and antelope at the water hole, had told him so. They were all creatures primarily of the veldt, and could not have been far from the open country that they favored.

Everyone started veering in that direction. He called, "No! Keep heading east; stay in the jungle!"

Even Penrod protested now. "The going will be much easier if we swing south!"

"It'll be easier for those who are following us, too," Tarzan said. "We can't go out on the veldt until we lose them."

So they stumbled on, still in the jungle. And suddenly Diana cried out in pain, slapping at her neck. Then all of them were shouting, beginning to scatter, slapping themselves with flailing arms.

They had encountered a cloud of flying ants, small black insects whose bite was like the jab of a red-hot needle.

This was his fault, Tarzan told himself. He had forgotten that he was immune to many things, and they were not. "Stop and fight them off as best you can," he called. "I'll be back in a moment."

He plunged aside, quickly scanning trees, and from one of them plucked something that looked like a pink cabbage. It was a parasitic plant that sucked liquid from the tree's trunk, and quite common. Tarzan returned with it, tearing away several of the leaves and crushing them between his hands. They exuded a thick, rubbery fluid.

"Rub this on your skin wherever it is exposed," he directed, passing the leaves among them.

Diana's nose wrinkled. "I don't like its smell!"

"It's either this or be bitten," Tarzan told her. "I use it. You may have noticed that the ants didn't bother me."

As soon as the insect repellent was well rubbed on he started them moving again, and its value was demonstrated only a little later when they passed a marshy depression where thousands of mosquitoes rose to meet them. They were not bitten.

Just past that place he called another halt and moved

ahead, treading warily. Dick Penrod was at his elbow. "Is something wrong?"

Tarzan pointed ahead to what seemed like a fat vine, mottled in brown and green, that hung from a tree.

Penrod said, "What is it?"

Tarzan picked up a stone and threw it. The vine suddenly writhed. A flat, ugly head appeared, with small unwinking eyes and the questing flicker of a forked tongue.

"Python," Tarzan explained. "A big one. I think he has fed recently, maybe a couple of days ago, and is still sluggish, not in a mood to want to bother any of us. But we won't take any chances. Swing wide. Give him plenty of room."

They worked around the huge snake. Diana shivered. Fletcher muttered, "Hawkins, put a bullet in the brute!"

Hawkins shrugged. "If I was to shoot everything that's liable to bother us, I'd soon be out of bullets."

Moments later Tarzan, still in the lead, stopped so suddenly that Penrod bumped into him. A swift swing of Tarzan's arm drove him back.

Diana said fretfully, "What is wrong now?"

"Be quiet, all of you," Tarzan ordered. "And listen!"

They were silent. What they heard was a faint, dusty-

sounding hiss. Then there was a sudden flash of movement on the ground. A snake that was as small around as a pencil, and not much longer, wriggled hurriedly away.

"That was Krait, the smallest of the vipers," Tarzan said. "His bite can be fatal very quickly. Listen for his hiss and if you hear it, jump out of the way as fast as you can."

If this were snake country, he thought, they could be in for serious trouble, particularly if Mamba, the black killer, lived in this stretch of jungle. Mamba could kill even faster and more surely than Krait, and was likely to attack instead of retreating.

But they worked on, and encountered no more snakes.

It was nearing midday now. They were soaked with perspiration, smeared with leaf-mold and dirt as well as a sort of green fungus that in spots covered the ground they walked on. Their clothing was tattered from rough usage.

All were limping, and Diana was beginning to complain of her blistered feet with almost every breath. But still Tarzan forced them to keep moving.

They were not yet far enough ahead of the Oparians. He had listened hard for drum talk from behind, but had not heard any. This drove him even harder. They might be all together, with no need to communicate with each other.

A game trail appeared, like the one Tarzan had investigated yesterday, a narrow path, probably centuries old, that cut through the jungle, probably leading from the veldt to a water hole. Tarzan waved the others across it and into the tangled greenery again.

Chetah, riding his back, was growing short-tempered. Too many branches and swinging vines were slapping her in the face. She tugged at Tarzan's hair, begging him to climb with her into the cool heights of the trees and to leave these other people to flounder on as best they could.

Tarzan said, "No." And then, "Little one, go back and take another look behind us."

Chetah grumbled at this, reluctant to swing into the trees without him. But she went.

And the nightmarish struggle through the jungle continued, until a moment somewhat later when he discovered that he, Dick Penrod, and Camage Dean were well out in front of the others.

He stopped, looking back. Hawkins, Fletcher, and Diana had stopped.

Tarzan turned back to them. Fletcher and Diana were sitting down; Diana was trying to get her shoes off.

"Don't do that, Mrs. Penrod. You won't be able to put

them on again," Tarzan said. "Get up. We have to go on."

"We've had all we can take," Fletcher said sullenly. "We're going to stay here until we're good and rested."

Hawkins was leaning on his rifle nearby. Tarzan glanced at him. "You talked them into this, Hawkins."

"So what if I did?" the lanky man growled. "It happens that I can't see any sense at all in keeping on like this. We've covered at least ten miles since leaving the canyon. It's far enough. There's no sign we're being trailed; and even if that pair we saw does manage to catch up with us, I'll handle them this time!"

He lifted his rifle meaningfully.

"Hawkins, you know I'm not running from that pair alone," Tarzan told him coldly.

Dick Penrod had left Camage Dean, a dozen yards away, and had come to join the group here. He frowned at this. "I had a feeling that was why you were pushing us so hard, Tarzan. You think there are more like those two?"

"Yes," Tarzan said. He had not wanted to tell them.

"Oh, maybe a few more," Hawkins conceded. "There was some drum-beating last night, late. I couldn't read much of it—they used a strange code—but even if there's as many as a dozen more of them, and they do manage to catch up, my gun will send them about their business."

Tarzan wondered how much truth there was in the man's words. But this was no time to attempt to find out. He said, "It's a lot smarter to get far enough away so there'll be no danger of them catching up. The only way we can be sure of doing that is to keep pushing on, as fast as possible."

"I think you're right. We can rest when there's a fair chance we'll be safe," Dick Penrod said, and reached down to help his wife up. "Diana, we have to go on."

She slapped petulantly at his hand, but Penrod got her to her feet. Fletcher grumbled but rose also.

While they had been talking, a sudden raucous clatter had begun all about them, with the arrival on the scene of a considerable number of monkeys.

There had been few of them around until now. Monkeys often gathered in large colonies for mutual protection. They had probably passed near one such colony, and a guard had notified the others, bringing them all in force to investigate; bringing also their characteristic musky odor, so thick and pungent that it muffled all other scents.

They swarmed thickly in the trees, black, brown, and gray, all sizes from tiny guenon monkeys to the big ones with red-tinted ruffs that were near kin to baboons. Tarzan even noticed several of the colobus, a rare and strange monkey, since it had only four fingers on its hand, with no thumb. A frail, gray creature, it had a fringe of hair about its face, so that it resembled an old woman peering through a shawl.

The din they made was earsplitting. Diana put both hands over her ears. "Can't you make them shut up?" she demanded of Tarzan.

He had to smile wryly. For the first minute or so, nothing could silence a monkey. During that time, as now, they devoted themselves to a boastful screaming that they were lords of the jungle and that no one could pass through it without their permission. But since no monkey could keep his mind on anything longer than that, the din would soon subside; they would start picking fleas from each other, or hunt something to eat, or just wander aimlessly away.

Their noise blocked off all other sounds, just as their rank odor prevented Tarzan from testing the jungle scents for those that might warn of danger. He caught Penrod's eye and pointed eastward, a signal for them to start moving and to get away from these pests.

But the monkey uproar suddenly grew louder, for Chetah was coming back.

Monkeys and chimpanzees heartily disliked each other,

something that probably went back to the beginning of time. Chetah usually refused to pay them any heed at all; she regarded monkeys, and rightly so, as scatterbrained idiots. But now they were screaming the ancient insult that she had no tail because it had been bitten off by baboons, and Chetah was screaming back in a furious rage.

Tarzan shouted, "Little one, forget about them! What did you see behind us?"

Chetah dropped from the trees. She waved both arms above her head, looking toward the east, and turned two swift somersaults before coming on toward Tarzan at her short-legged, lumbering run.

She had warned of danger, immediate and near. But it was not behind them. And still that tumult continued.

Tarzan filled his lungs and sent his call at the noisy pests: *"Ah-ee-ahhhh!"*

It shocked the monkeys to instant silence and sent them scrambling away in headlong, fearful flight.

Tarzan tested the clearing air with his nostrils, head lifted, and found the scent he had detected yesterday on the game trail. His ears caught the rustle of secretive movement nearby.

The moments those monkeys had been here had been

nearly fatal, and might be yet. Chetah had warned of two men closing in. But they were not behind; they must have taken to that game trail, running fast to get in front and to attack from that direction. They were coming from the east.

Tarzan whirled toward Camage Dean as she cried out and tried to run; at the last moment she had realized that she was in danger.

It was too late. The Oparian spearman they had seen at the canyon broke from cover and leaped at her. He seized the woman, an arm whipping about her from behind, and held her as a shield. His spear lifted, held short on the shaft; its point touched her throat.

"Jambo, m-tu zanje!" he shouted at Tarzan. "Make no move, or the woman dies!"

Then the second one appeared, the same who had fired those arrows at the canyon. He had his bow ready, an arrow notched and drawn back.

That arrow was aimed directly at Tarzan. The bowman cat-footed toward him, scarred face showing a triumphant grimace.

"Your blood is for drinking at Opar, white man," he said. "But stand still or I will drink it here!"

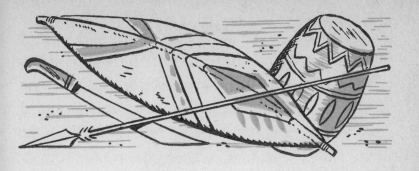

Chapter 7   Trail Without End

The bowman stopped, half a dozen paces away. At such a distance a miss seemed impossible if he should let his arrow fly.

There was deep quiet. Camage Dean stood rigid, in the grip of the other Oparian. As the stillness continued, Tarzan heard Diana breathing raggedly. He hoped she would not suddenly become hysterical.

Tarzan dropped the bundles he was carrying. Chetah came ambling along, paying him no attention at all. She poked into the things she had brought from the plane, dug out the heavy brass ring, held it so it glittered in the sunlight, then leaped into the trees, carying the ring along.

The bowman turned part of his attention toward her, frowning. Tarzan spoke quickly: "What do you wish of us?"

"You speak our tongue!" the Oparian said, forgetting Chetah. *"Bom!* Good! Now stay very still, and tell the others to do the same. We will wait until the rest of the searchers come along."

"I got that!" Hawkins exclaimed. He held his rifle in one hand now, with its muzzle pointing toward the ground. "And we've got to do like he says, make no move at all, or it's Miss Dean's finish. Tarzan, don't you go trying anything foolish! We'll just have to stand quiet until the rest of their bunch shows up. Maybe I can talk them into letting us pay a ransom to go free—"

"Y-Yes!" Diana Penrod gasped. "Promise anything; I'll pay it!"

Tarzan felt grim amusement. All that Diana Penrod owned in worldly goods would not be enough to buy them freedom. And Hawkins was a fool if he believed otherwise.

The bowman spoke suspiciously: "What words are they saying?"

"They are agreeing to do as you ordered," Tarzan told him. Then, "How many are the rest of the searchers that follow after you?"

"More than twice the number of your fingers, white man!" the Oparian answered.

"Have you all survived the ordeal of the seven days of torture?" Tarzan asked.

"Arghh!" the other said, a lionlike growl of boastfulness. "Yes! We walked the path of fire, endured the whippings, and made no sounds. There were many who failed, but the blood gods gave the rest of us courage, and Ogonooroo sent us forth on this search."

Tarzan remembered that Hawkins had spoken of Ogonooroo as a fat, stupid fool, chief at Opar. Hawkins had claimed he planned to trade him cheap trinkets for valuable ivory. But a chief who used torture as a means of determining the strongest and fiercest men in his tribe did not sound very stupid.

Had Hawkins been lying, or had he been tricked by Ogonooroo, who had played stupid in the hope Hawkins would return to Opar, bringing other whites with him?

The bowman went on, "We will have much glory when we reach Opar, taking you whites with us!"

"The most glory should be yours. You are a very brave warrior," Tarzan said, still using the mixture of Swahili and Ivory Coast dialect they were speaking.

It was talk meant to keep the attention of both Oparians concentrated on him. From a corner of his eye Tarzan was watching the trees above and beyond the warrior who was holding his spear-point against the throat of Camage Dean. A slight shaking of foliage was momentarily visible there.

"You are right," the bowman agreed. "I should be made a chief of at least ten warriors as my reward for capturing you, the white man who flies through trees, who has a voice like thunder and the strength of ten men. Arghh! I shall drink your blood on the night of sacrifice; it will give me your strength!"

Chetah plummeted straight down from the trees, landing on the back of the spearman. And as she landed, she swung the heavy brass ring at his head.

It struck with a sharp chunking sound. The man, instantly unconscious, went sideways and down, a hard fall to the ground, dragging Camage Dean with him.

Tarzan leaped at the bowman, crouched low, charging straight at him, a streaking rush faster than any creature of the jungle could match.

Nothing, however, could move fast enough to reach the Oparian before he released his arrow. The string of the horn bow twanged, with a humming sound, and the arrow flashed at Tarzan.

Because he was crouched low, it missed his head by

inches. Then they crashed together. The Oparian dropped his bow. His hands gripped Tarzan's throat, digging deep.

There was great strength in the man, iron in his hands and cunning in his gouging thumbs. It was a throttling hold that could render any ordinary man helpless in seconds.

But the ridged muscles of Tarzan's throat ignored the fierce pressure of those fingers. Tarzan's hands gripped the man's body; he jerked his feet clear of the ground and lifted him, a move that broke the other's hold on his throat. At the same time it twisted and wrenched the Oparian with a violence that made the bronze-colored warrior, who had endured brutal pagan torture in silence, cry out painfully.

Tarzan slammed the Oparian down flat, a bruising, bone-shaking fall against the earth. He bent, clamped both hands on him and lifted him again, holding the man so his toes barely touched the ground, and shook him hard.

"Imshi! Talk quickly, before I shake your bones apart!" Tarzan said. "Where is Opar? What direction and how far? Tell me that first, and then of the sacrifices at the last blood moon—"

The harsh, flat crack of a rifle interrupted him, and the

Oparian, hit by Hawkins' bullet, became a dead weight, senseless, dangling in Tarzan's grip.

He let the man go, to spill down in a huddled heap, and wheeled about to face Hawkins, who still had his rifle partially raised, a wisp of smoke curling away from its muzzle.

The lanky man swallowed, with a contrite look. "Shouldn't have done that, Tarzan," he said quickly. "Kind of got excited, I guess, everything happening so fast—and his arrow nearly skewered me. I pulled trigger at him without thinking. I'm sorry."

No man who had hunted big game, facing the charges of lions, rhino, and buffalo, would have grown excited at the near flight of an arrow. But, Tarzan thought, perhaps he was giving Hawkins too much credit. The man was also said to have poisoned elephants for their ivory, which was the most cowardly form of murder in Africa. He might have become panicky and fired without thinking, just as he had said.

If so, he might do it again. Tarzan said, "Hawkins, give me your rifle."

Hawkins went back a step, starting to swing the muzzle of his gun toward Tarzan. "Now, wait a minute!"

There was no time for argument. Tarzan went at him, another move almost too swift to follow, and wrenched the Mannlicher from Hawkins' hands. He worked its ejector swiftly, pumping shells from the gun's magazine until it was empty, catching them in his hand.

He threw the unloaded rifle back at Hawkins, who caught it awkwardly. Tarzan held out the shells. "Put these in your jacket pocket. Carry the gun empty so you won't make any more mistakes with it."

Hawkins chewed his lip but he did not speak. Tarzan turned for an examination of the Oparian who had been hit by that hurriedly fired bullet.

Diana's fingers fluttered against her mouth. "Is—is he—"

"No," Tarzan answered. "It wasn't a fatal hit, but he'll probably be unconscious for some minutes."

He went then to look at the other Oparian. Camage was on her feet, very pale but steady. Tarzan spoke gently to her. "You're all right, Miss Dean?"

"Yes," she answered. "I was afraid, of course, but I told myself not to be, that you would do something to—to get us all free."

The Oparian who had seized her was still senseless. Chetah was capering proudly about, waving the metal ring back and forth over her head.

Dick Penrod said, "Tarzan, did you—well, tell her to get that ring and do what she did?"

Tarzan glanced at Chetah for a moment, recalling how she had first come to him, a baby chimp from the dark Ruwenzori forest, how she had attached herself to him, going wherever he went, refusing to be shooed away, frequently a nuisance, even to this day, with her inquisitiveness and almost-human tantrums. What she had just done more than made up for all the exasperations Chetah had ever caused.

"I didn't have a chance to tell her anything," Tarzan answered. "She figured it all out on her own, and don't ask me how. Chetah is constantly doing things for which there is no explanation."

"Well, she did a lot to get us out of a very tight spot, and I'm plenty grateful," Penrod said. He bent down, offering his hand to Chetah. "Shake, pardner!"

Chetah solemnly shook hands, bobbing her head, with a chattering remark that might have been the chimpanzee equivalent of, "Oh, it wasn't anything, really!"

Camage said, "I'd like to shake her hand, too."

Before she could do so, however, Diana spoke fretfully:

"Camage, come here! I need you. That was such a terrible ordeal for me; I think I'm going to faint."

Camage stiffened, sudden bright spots of color flaring in her cheeks. Her lips worked indignantly. Before she could speak, Tarzan said to her, low-voiced, "Please go and help Mrs. Penrod get started. We must move on at once."

He nodded to Dick Penrod, who turned and plunged into the jungle tangles, beginning once again to beat a path through them.

Tarzan picked up the horn bow dropped by the Oparian whom Hawkins had shot, and broke it in half. He did the same with the spear of the one Chetah had downed, who was now beginning to stir and mutter dazedly. Tarzan paid him no heed.

"Hawkins, go and help Penrod," he ordered. "You, too, Fletcher."

Hawkins said, voice sly, "Kind of foolish, leaving them like this, when you could make real sure they won't ever bother us again."

Tarzan studied him coldly, disdaining to say that he had never taken advantage of any man unable to defend himself, no matter what circumstances might seem to excuse such action, and was not beginning now.

"Those others will be along soon; that shot you fired will bring them on a beeline, Hawkins," he said. "Get going!"

They struggled on through breathless afternoon heat, mile after slow mile, always in the thick jungle undergrowth which was at times matted like hedgerows and apparently as impenetrable. But Tarzan showed them how to find the spots where they could break through, close to forest giants where the lush green growth thinned out just a little.

Such travel did not weary him, nor did it begin to tire Hawkins, accustomed to the hard life of the veldt, for quite a while. But the others, softened by civilized living, were put to a grim test that afternoon. They had to keep going, up to the limits of their endurance—and beyond.

Tarzan regretted the necessity for such hard driving. But he knew these people could withstand much more than they thought they could, and it must be done now. In them, as in all humans, were deep reservoirs of unsuspected strength, available for dire emergencies like this one. He forced them to call upon that strength and to use it.

Tarzan did not permit a rest stop for some time. Then

he allowed them a sparing drink again, and broke up one of the chocolate bars into small equal parts which gave each a portion to munch. Fletcher demanded more than that. "You've got a whole box; I saw them!" he croaked.

"And they'll be needed later," Tarzan told him. "That's all you get for now."

He ate none of the chocolate himself, but gave a sliver to Chetah, who loved everything sweet.

Fletcher objected bitterly to that, and also to Tarzan giving Chetah a drink from the flask. "Let your ape drink out of one of the mud holes we keep passing!" he said.

It was true enough they had encountered a number of small seeps—muddy, stagnant water. Tarzan did not bother to answer Fletcher's tirade, but Camage Dean did.

"Hal, why don't you shut up?" she said spiritedly. "All you do is complain, and it doesn't help things a bit!"

Fletcher stared at her, too amazed by her sudden show of spunk to say anything. Tarzan announced, "Everybody up! We're moving on."

And so the day stretched out, with the sun seeming to hang motionless in the sky before it finally began to slide down toward the western horizon. There was somnolent quiet in the jungle at this hour, with birds roosting sleepily, monkeys dozing, the predatory beasts in their cool haunts.

Chetah had accompanied Dick Penrod for some time. Then she came back to ride on Tarzan's shoulders. Obeying the primitive law of the jungle that this was the time of day for napping, she even dozed a little herself, arms wrapped about his neck.

Now she came awake with a sudden brisk chirping. Tarzan nodded. "All right. Go and see what is ahead of us. But do not go too far."

She flew away through the trees.

The silence continued, broken only by hard breathing, muffled exclamations, the scrape of footsteps, as all of them pushed forward.

No rattle of drums echoed behind them, although it had been hours since they had left the two Oparians. Tarzan had expected them to be found, had expected a quick message informing the other warriors scattered through the jungle of that. But there had been no such message.

It might be they had shaken off those pursuers. However, that couldn't be taken for granted yet.

Penrod suddenly cried out in surprise. Tarzan went quickly to the head of the line to join him.

They had come upon a river, a narrow, muddy stream

that moved at a sluggish pace between low banks, with the trees on either side almost touching over the slow current.

Hawkins came to have a look also. "Better work downstream, and not try to cross it," he said. "There are croc tracks around."

"Yes, but not many," Tarzan said. "And none of the beasts in sight. A few probably wandered upstream, found it too shallow here, and went back."

Crocodiles favored fairly deep water because of their practice of dragging prey underwater to drown it.

"You and I will take the lead, Hawkins," Tarzan said. "The rest of you, follow close behind us."

Hawkins made a sour face, but plunged into the river. The crossing was made without incident. The water was only about waist-deep on the women.

Hawkins was beginning to tire noticeably now. The others stumbled along in a haze of fatigue, one slow step after another.

Beyond that river the jungle began to thin out again. Then Chetah reappeared, dropping to Tarzan's shoulders. She jumped about in great excitement, smacking her lips and pointing ahead.

"There's water nearby," Tarzan said. "A clear stream

or a lake. Chetah didn't pay any attention to the river, because she won't drink muddy water."

This with a glance at Hal Fletcher, who curled a lip but was too tired to say anything.

Then they broke from the last of the jungle, with open country before them—and, in the near distance, a blue glitter of water. It was a lake, stretching off out of sight toward the north, a mile or more wide.

"All of you, wait here," Tarzan said. "I'll go ahead, find a good place to camp, fill both of the flasks, and come back. With water like that, there'll be plenty of game, plenty to eat tonight—"

His voice died. They were stretched out on the ground in various completely relaxed postures, utterly spent, with no interest in anything he might say. Even Hawkins had sat down, drawn up his knees, and had his head against them. His rifle, forgotten, was in the dust beside him.

Chapter 8   **Kidnaped!**

At sunrise the next morning Tarzan stirred and rose, stretching, breathing deeply, then bent to add fuel to the small fire, building it up carefully, using wood that burned with little or no smoke.

Perhaps it was an unnecessary precaution. There had been drum talk last night, but only briefly, late, after the others were fast asleep—a sound rather distant. Tarzan could not make out what was being said. That it was at some distance had been encouraging.

The Oparians would undoubtedly come on, with the dawn of this new day, but their quarry would be traveling again, also. If the lead that had been obtained could be retained and increased, there was a fairly good chance the Oparians never would catch up.

Three figures huddled in deep motionless slumber beside the fire—Penrod, Fletcher, and Hawkins. Tarzan had chosen as the spot for this camp a place at the base of a low sandstone cliff about a quarter of a mile from the lake.

Nearby, but secluded, was a lean-to he had built for the women, granting them some privacy since it was possible to do so, poles slanted against the cliff and thatched with grass that grew near the lake's margin.

Tarzan had brought them all here at sunset last night, a slow, straggling procession. He had set up the camp, had gone northward along the lake for a brief hunt, and presently the haunch of a small bush gazelle was roasting over glowing coals. Tarzan had also found a plant whose roots, baked in ashes, had a squashlike taste. One of the tins of English biscuits had completed the meal; and in spite of their weariness the five had eaten heartily, once it was ready.

Tarzan left the camp this bright new morning, and headed toward the nearby lake. A herd of sitatunga, fifty or more, grazing in the grass along its edge, suddenly whirled with flashing tails and ran from him. They were water antelope, found only along the margins of lakes or large rivers. They plunged into the lake and swam strongly, heading across it.

Sitatunga had strange, elongated hoofs, which made them very good swimmers. Tarzan paused for a moment, watching them. He heard a call from behind, and looked around to see Chetah following him at a hurried scramble, protesting because he had not invited her along on this morning excursion.

"I didn't think you wanted to be bothered," Tarzan said. "You were curled up there beside Penrod; I thought you were waiting until he awakened so you could plague him for his lighter again."

Chetah had begged for the lighter last night and had snapped it in absorbed fascination, again and again.

"It works on butane and is good for a thousand lights," Penrod had told Tarzan. "I don't mind her playing with it, as long as she isn't liable to hurt herself."

That wasn't likely to happen. Chetah knew all about fire, and she had a healthy respect for it. She knew all about matches, too, but had never displayed any great interest in them. It was the lighter's bright glitter, as well as the fact that she could make flame spurt from it, that fascinated her.

Chetah started now to explain that she had curled up beside Penrod only because he was closer to the fire than

Tarzan, and she hadn't really been thinking very much about begging for the lighter as soon as Penrod awakened. It was an explanation that became involved, with much chirping and arm-waving, and was interrupted by the sudden appearance of half a dozen small gray rock apes.

They yelped a greeting to Chetah and capered about in friendly fashion, welcoming this close cousin. Chetah, seizing the opportunity to end talk about the lighter—she was afraid Tarzan would order her not to play with it any more—rushed at the apes with teeth bared, barking an opinion that they were only rather large monkeys, and for them to be off about their business.

This move was a bad mistake. The rock apes promptly began to pelt her with stones, and their aim was dismayingly accurate. Chetah came hurrying back to Tarzan, arms wrapped about her head to protect it, yelling in pain as some of the stones hit her.

She got Tarzan between herself and the apes, and crouched there, muttering woefully as she rubbed her bruises.

"You asked for it, so don't come to me for sympathy," Tarzan said. Then he clucked soothingly to the apes, who stopped throwing stones and huddled together, staring at him, recognizing the tones they heard, somewhat frightened because a man-thing spoke to them. They decided to go away, and did.

Tarzan went on to the edge of the lake.

It was still and placid, ruffled only by the swimming sitatunga. Beyond it the land lifted in long barren rises toward the distant mountains that were now a dim, hazy blue against the horizon.

At the south end of the lake, several miles away, some low brown hills began, rising above rather thick patches of timber along the shore. They would have to cut through those hills this morning, Tarzan told himself, in their southeastward slant toward the distant Ngamu River.

Chetah continued to mutter and rub herself. Then she forgot about her bruises as Tarzan stepped down to the edge of the lake's blue water and poised himself, arms lifted high. She chattered a protest.

He left the land in a long dive that cut the water like a knife-edge, came up quickly, and began to swim toward the center of the lake.

Chetah bounced up and down, crying out in disapproval. She could swim very well if necessary, but greatly disliked getting wet and could never understand Tarzan going into water when there was no need to do so.

He swam with a strong overhand crawl. Tarzan had figured out that swimming stroke for himself, as a small dog-paddling foster son of the great apes—who had also been puzzled and concerned by his liking for water—long before he knew there were creatures in the world like himself that swam in the same manner.

The water was cool and exhilarating. Well out toward the middle of the narrow lake, Tarzan abruptly twisted and went under, going deep into blue depths, looking about.

He came up again minutes later—four minutes later, actually, and nowhere near exhaustion of the air stored in his great chest, and swam back to land. An onlooker might have noted that he moved at a somewhat faster pace, returning.

Chetah had withdrawn a little from the water's edge, with a wary eye on Diana Penrod, who had appeared there.

The young woman waited until Tarzan had left the lake and was shaking himself, before she spoke: "The water looks very nice. If you'll go away now, I'll have a swim also—"

"I'm sorry," Tarzan said. "You can't swim here. It's too dangerous."

She sniffed, looking about at the placid lake, the deserted shore line. "Just what is going to harm me? I don't see any crocodiles. Or perhaps you're going to tell me I'll be bitten by water snakes?"

Tarzan shook his head. "There aren't any crocs here; they like muddier, more stagnant water. And you might encounter water snakes, though they're not harmful—"

Diana tossed her head. "Well, what could be out in the lake then, that might be dangerous?"

"Hippos," Tarzan told her. "They're walking on the bottom, feeding. I counted about a dozen of them, all big ones, due to surface for air at any moment. They might not pay you any heed at all—or might bite your legs off, since they've been known to do so."

Diana had been listening in growing disbelief. She stamped her foot, interrupting him: "Do you take me for a complete fool? Hippos walking on the bottom—feeding —I never heard such utter nonsense!"

Out in the lake, about fifty yards from shore, a great glistening head suddenly appeared above the surface. Dull, piggish eyes stared at them. A cavernous mouth opened, showing blunt yellowed tusks, and snapped shut again with a sound like the slamming of a door.

Water boiled as the others appeared, a dozen of them in all, as Tarzan had said there would be. Small ears moving loosely, slate-colored hide wrinkling in the early sunshine, they grunted and squealed together.

Diana's face had gone pale. She stared at them in amazement. "They really were on the bottom?"

Tarzan nodded. He had seen them in the lake's blue depths when he had gone under. It was one of the rarest sights in Africa.

"They are very fond of submerged water plants," he said. "Some scientists claim they can stay under only up to a limit of about eight minutes, but these must have been on the bottom for ten or twelve minutes, at least. I came back as soon as I saw them. The hippo is too big and short-tempered for anyone to take any chances with him. We'd better leave before they take it into their heads to come ashore; they can move faster than you might think. And I'm sorry you had to miss your swim—"

Diana shivered. "Never mind," she said. "I've lost all desire for that!"

Diana returned to the lean-to to wake up Camage Dean. Tarzan went on to the fire.

Dick Penrod was up and moving about. Hawkins was using a strip of red cloth from Tarzan's bundle to clean his rifle. Hal Fletcher was still dozing, or seeming to; Tarzan nudged him with a foot. "Get up, Fletcher, and put your clothes on. The women will soon be joining us, and we'll move out as soon as we've eaten."

Fletcher sat up, yawning and scowling. He and Penrod had washed their clothes at the lake last night after supper; so had the women, but at a different place. Hawkins hadn't bothered. From his looks, the hunter had never formed a very strong habit of washing either himself or his clothes.

Hal Fletcher had hung his outer garments to dry on a stunted salt bush nearby. He made no immediate move toward them but stretched, grimacing.

"I'm creaky and sore in every muscle," he muttered sourly. "Can't we stay here today, rest up before going on?"

"No," Tarzan said, kneeling beside the bundle he had brought through the jungle yesterday, beginning to sort out its contents.

Fletcher looked to Hawkins, with a gesture that begged for his support in opposing Tarzan's plan to move on.

Another gazelle haunch that Tarzan had set to roast

beside the fire about three that morning was crusty brown and dripping fat with a sizzling sound on the coals beneath. Dick Penrod was using a stick to dig out the roots that had also been set to bake in hot ashes.

Tarzan was arranging in four equal piles the food items he had taken from the plane. He glanced at Dick Penrod. "Will you hunt around and get me four sticks about like the one you're using, please?"

Penrod nodded and went off to search for them. When he came back, Tarzan had used the drapes he had taken from the plane windows to make four bags. He had filled them and tied them up, with knots through which he now thrust the four sticks. Penrod grinned. "Looks like you're fixing a hobo bindle for each of us to carry," he remarked.

Tarzan smiled. "Yes. In South Africa it is called a sundowner's swag. A sundowner is a tramp who tries to live without working, and who appears just at sundown, after all the evening chores are finished, to beg a meal. He carries his possessions wrapped up in a bag and carried on a stick over his shoulder."

"Just like an American hobo!" Penrod laughed. "And we're going to carry those bindles from now on?"

Tarzan nodded. "If for any reason we should become

separated, each of you will have emergency food rations. Fortunately, the tins of beef and biscuits have keys attached which will open them. I have also divided up the chocolate bars among you. I have made only four of the bags, since Hawkins must keep his hands free to handle his rifle if necessary."

Penrod lifted one of the bindles and swung it experimentally over his shoulder. "Not very heavy; we shouldn't have any trouble packing them," he decided.

Chetah tugged at Tarzan's arm with a pleading sound, then grabbed at the stick of one of the other bindles and tried to sling it over her shoulder, imitating Dick Penrod. But its weight was too much for a small chimpanzee; it jerked her backward and she sat down on the ground, hard.

Penrod chuckled. "It looks like you'll have to make her a bindle to carry, too," he remarked.

"I won't get any peace until I do," Tarzan agreed. "See if you can find me another stick."

He made a small bindle, put the heavy brass ring into it, thrust a stick through the knot, and handed it to Chetah. She slung it over her shoulder and marched about the fire, eager to begin the day's trek.

"We aren't leaving yet," Penrod said, and offered her

his lighter. "Here, play with this."

Chetah showed her teeth in a pleased grin and began to wander about, snapping the lighter, blowing out the flame, and snapping it again.

Fletcher's lip curled. "All that trouble to keep a silly monkey happy!" he said.

Tarzan unrolled the leopard skin and began to cut strips from it, a first step in the making of moccasins for the two women. Hawkins cleared his throat.

"Maybe Fletcher is right about all of us resting up some here, if only for a couple of hours," he said.

Tarzan sent a piercing stare at the man. "Hawkins, you should know we're far from out of danger. And there's something I want to know right now—"

What he wanted to know was why Hawkins was trying again to hold them back. But a sudden howl of rage from Fletcher interrupted him. Chetah had wandered too close to the salt bush, which was tinder dry, and had managed accidentally to set it on fire. The bush was burning with a crackling sound, and so were Fletcher's clothes, hung on it.

Fletcher ran at Chetah, trying to grab her. She dodged him, still holding the bindle over her shoulder, gripping the lighter in one hand. Fletcher chased Chetah around the fire, shouting in anger and shaking his fist.

Tarzan, meanwhile, reached the salt bush in two long strides, plucked off Fletcher's shirt, jacket, and trousers, and slapped them against the ground, quickly beating out the fire in them.

Fletcher, still pursuing Chetah, bent and snatched up a heavy rock. He lifted it to throw at her. Tarzan got between the two of them. Fletcher ran into him and bounced back.

"That's enough," Tarzan told him.

"Get out of my way! I'll teach that meddling ape a lesson!" Fletcher panted.

"No, you won't," Tarzan said. "I apologize for what she did—though it was an accident. And if you had put your clothes on when I told you to, it wouldn't have happened. Go and put them on now. The women are coming."

Fletcher glared at him. But Tarzan's commanding gaze made him drop his eyes. The man turned away, chewed his lip, and sullenly began to pull on his trousers. The legs had been burned off up to his knees. His jacket and shirt were only scorched.

Hawkins was openly grinning, and Penrod was repressing a smile. Fletcher cut a comic figure at that, Tarzan thought, and perhaps it served him right for his laziness and unpleasant remarks.

But that was no reason to ignore what had happened. Tarzan called, "Chetah, bring me the lighter."

She tried to shuffle away, pretending she had not heard him.

Tarzan said, "No, that won't work. Bring it here."

Chetah reluctantly obeyed, mumbling apologetically, promising she would not be careless with the lighter again.

"I can't take a chance on that," Tarzan said, tossing the lighter to Penrod. "Burning things is bad, no matter how it happens. You're not to play with the fire-maker again."

Then he turned his attention back to Hawkins, but before he could speak, Camage Dean appeared on the scene.

She stared at the burning salt bush, and at Hal Fletcher. "Whatever has been happening here?" Camage asked.

Tarzan looked past her, toward the lean-to. Nobody was there. "Miss Dean, where is Mrs. Penrod?" he asked.

"Why, she hasn't been with me," Camage said. "I thought that I'd find her here."

There was sudden stillness by the fire.

"When did you see her last?" Tarzan asked.

"About half an hour ago. Diana discovered her jacket

was missing, and thought she must have left it where we washed our clothes last night. She said she would go to the lake and get it."

Tarzan looked toward the lake. Diana Penrod was not in sight.

He swung his gaze toward the south. This low sandstone cliff ended about half a mile away. Beyond it some fairly thick timber began. Studying the trees there intently, Tarzan saw a sudden flash of light. It was a brief glint of sunshine against metal.

In the same instant he heard a distant, fearful cry that was abruptly cut off short.

An exclamation was wrenched from Dick Penrod: "Diana!" He took a couple of strides in that direction before Tarzan's hand on his arm jerked him to a halt.

He had discovered the source of that flash of light. It was the iron point of an Oparian spear. Now, narrowing his gaze down, Tarzan saw them yonder.

There were two of the warriors fading among the trees, both bearing shields and spears—and two more beyond them, carrying Diana's limp body. She seemed to be unconscious. Tarzan had only one quick glimpse before they disappeared.

If all the Oparians had reached the lake, he told himself, there would have been an attack rather than the seizure of one captive. So those four must have been sent ahead as scouts. They had caught Diana wandering alone near the lake, and were hurrying her back to the main body of warriors.

There was a good chance to head them off before they could reach the others. Tarzan said, "I'll go after them! All of you, wait here!"

Then he was gone, at a long, running stride, racing along the base of the cliff, reaching those trees and swerving in among them, heading westward after the retreating Oparians.

Chapter 9   River of Crocodiles

It was forest growth too thin for Tarzan to swing into the branches and increase his speed. He had to stay on the ground.

These were trees of the veldt, growing here at the edge of the jungle: plane trees with their strange, flattened tops, acacias, various species of thorn trees. Tarzan ran among them, keeping to cover as much as possible. There was some brush, brown and dry, and the ground was powdery underfoot; it had been months since the last rain season.

The four Oparians had left a plain trail which he followed swiftly. But they had moved in a hurry, also; Tarzan had no glimpse of them. A mile passed, and another. From some distance he heard the brief rattle of a drum, sounding the questioning call. There was no answer.

Then the character of the land suddenly changed, almost within a dozen strides, and at the same time Tarzan lost the tracks he had been following. The undergrowth became thicker and greener, and the familiar trees of the jungle began to appear again.

He cast back and forth hurriedly, trying to pick up their spoor again, and could not. They had vanished into the thickening mass of greenery. Tarzan gave up trying to track by sight—and a familiar, thickening, sour stench in the air made following them by scent impossible. He moved straight ahead with wariness, broke through a fringe of tangled vines, and found that he was looking down at the same river that had been crossed yesterday.

Its banks here were from thirty to fifty feet high. The river swirled slowly along beneath him, and the source of that sour stench was revealed: crocodiles, dozens and hundreds of them, some floating in the river with only their snouts and evil eyes above the surface, many sunning themselves torpidly on mud flats that appeared on both sides of the river at water level.

Tarzan paused a moment, looking and listening. The channel below was narrow, though it looked deep. He heard the rattle of that drum again, much closer than before. This time there was a prompt reply.

It came from across the channel, a swift, stuttering burst of sound. A white had been seized, the message said, but the other whites were probably running. They could be caught before the sun was very high if followed swiftly.

Tarzan frowned as he read the drumbeat code. The four Oparians must have acted very quickly; they must have crossed the river with Diana to the western bank, though Tarzan with a quick survey could not see where they had managed to get down, or up, the high banks of the channel. However, the drum talk seemed to indicate plainly that she was now over there.

And a dangerous thing to involve her in, since such a crossing must have been made on logs. Tarzan looked down at the great lizardlike beasts in the river and on the mud flats with anger as he thought of a woman being recklessly exposed to attack by them.

Of the few forms of life in Africa which Tarzan thought might well be eliminated, crocodiles stood high on the list. Cruel, wanton killers, they served no good whatever.

But this was no time to think of such a thing. If he moved fast enough, he could still catch up with those four Oparian scouts before the other warriors joined them.

Tarzan went up a high gum tree, selecting a liana and

taking it with him. On a lofty branch he paused a moment, studying the distance across to the western bank with hard concentration. Then, gripping the vine, he leaped out and down, swinging far over the stream. But he did not let go. Instead he swung back again, whipping himself through a long arc, using the vine as a circus performer might use a trapeze, hurtling far out over the river again, then back.

The third time, at the very top of his swing, a good hundred feet above the water, he let go and flew through space, spanning the channel in one gigantic effort.

The west bank was somewhat lower than the one on the eastern side. Tarzan had picked a dead tree as his target, one that stood tall and gaunt, with bare limbs. He caught one of those limbs with reaching hands and gripped hard, whipping himself around in a complete giant turn before the momentum of his leap could be halted. Then he hung there for a moment, looking from that lofty perch—and discovered he had made a mistake.

He had not reached the river's west bank. From this vantage point Tarzan could see that he was, instead, on a long, narrow island. The river had split against it a mile northward, with channels flowing down both sides.

But that drum talk he had heard had come from this

island. What did it mean? The four Oparians would not have crossed both channels, then returned to the island again. The answer seemed plain enough. Those four, with Diana, were still on the east side of the river. There were other Oparians below Tarzan on the island.

Tarzan glanced toward the east bank which he had just left, and shook his head; he could not swing back to that higher bank. And he could not stay where he was, either. The island timber was too thin to offer him any sanctuary in the trees.

He dropped swiftly down through the branches of the dead tree—but, quickly as he moved, the Oparians moved even faster. An arrow whistled close to him, and another. Grimly triumphant yells sounded. They came at Tarzan with a rush as he reached the ground.

Three of them were in the lead, charging from high brown saw grass. One was out in front of the others, a bronzed giant with muscles like knotted ropes, his skin glittering in the hot morning sun as though it had been oiled. He drove at Tarzan with a ferocious shout.

Tarzan moved back as though to give ground. But this was only a feint. Then he leaped at the warrior, a move swifter than the killing charge of Numa the lion.

His powerful hands clamped the man's body, jerked him off his feet, and lifted him high, at arm's length overhead. The pair following close behind him tried to stop, eyes bulging in amazement at that feat of strength. Tarzan threw the man he held at them, there was a crunching collision of flesh and bone, and the two, hit by that flying body, went down like tenpins.

But this move gained him only temporary respite. More arrows were flying; more Oparians were charging through the saw grass. Tarzan whirled and ran toward the south end of the island, the only way open to him.

The Oparians followed fast, closing in with a din of yelling. He had been right, Tarzan thought, in his surmise that they would not fight their way through the jungle by night, or they would have been here even before this. But they must have taken up the trail at this morning's first light, and luck must have favored them; they had probably found a game trail that led directly to this island, where they had made the same mistake he had, crossing to it with the thought they were fording the river.

Luck did not favor Tarzan. The Oparians pressed him hard, a line of warriors that was quickly extended until it stretched completely across the narrow island. Glancing back, Tarzan counted them—nine in all. No, an even dozen; the three he had momentarily disposed of had picked themselves up and were joining in this pursuit. Still more of them were somewhere west of the river. The drum had called to them to come on in a hurry.

No more arrows were fired. No spears were thrown. Tarzan heard the deep bellow of a voice shouting harsh orders: "Take the white devil alive! Save his blood for the gods of Opar!"

The island ended at its southern extremity in a narrow, tapering point of land. Here the two channels of the river came together again. Tarzan stopped at this point.

He saw a sheer drop below him, forty or more feet down to the river. And the crocodiles were gathering there, milling about, churning the muddy water to froth. Perhaps they were only excited by the fierce, exultant yelling of the warriors, though some primitive instinct always seemed to bring them when there was a possibility that something would be delivered to their gaping maws.

Tarzan faced about.

The Oparians were closing in on him, almost shoulder to shoulder now, brandishing bows, rattling spears against their lifted shields.

Tarzan's hand gripped his knife, still sheathed at his side, though he realized well enough it would not help much against the approaching warriors. Odds of twelve against one were too great for any man to face, no matter how much strength or fighting ability he might possess.

That deep, bellowing voice he had heard previously shouted an order, and the line of warriors halted about twenty feet from him. A man stepped forward in front of them. He halted also, facing Tarzan.

He was of massive build, with bulging muscles in his arms and shoulders. He wore a headdress of scarlet and green feathers, and a carved ivory medallion as big as a soup plate hung around his neck on a crudely worked copper chain. His face was like a mask, so many deep scars crisscrossed it; his eyes glittered among those scars, cold and malignant. He wore an air of brutal authority.

"*M-tu zanje,* I have been told you understand the words we speak," he growled.

"You must have learned that from the two I left behind for you yesterday," Tarzan said.

"Yes," the other admitted. "Those two dishonored the vows they took, during the seven days of torture, by letting you overcome them. They will never see Opar again."

These people, Tarzan realized, were even more merciless than he had yet figured them. A savage rumble from the other warriors indicated they approved that ruthlessness.

"Hear me!" the other continued. "I am Waziru. Only Ogonooroo is a greater chief than I, in Opar. Three times have I endured the seven days of torture, more than any other man. I have sworn to take you as my prisoner. Throw down your knife and surrender!"

This Waziru was obviously in command of the warriors here, and of those nearby. Tarzan wondered how many more of them there were.

Waziru continued, with a grimace that was probably meant as a wicked grin, "There are no trees here; you cannot leap into the branches and fly away. And—" he gestured toward the river which was now boiling with activity "—unless you join the crocodiles, you have no other choice. Do as I say—surrender!"

The answer to this was a measuring stare from eyes even colder than Waziru's. "I am Tarzan, lord of the jungle, known to people in far lands and in cities that are a thousand thousand times greater than the collection of huts you call Opar. I have faced in combat more warriors than you have ever seen, each greater than you, and conquered them all. I will never surrender!"

Waziru's mouth had begun to work convulsively midway in Tarzan's speech. Each of those words had stung his arrogant pride, which was Tarzan's intention.

"Four of my warriors have seized a white woman," Waziru said. "We have you, and we will soon seize the others. But first, I will make you squirm in the dirt!"

He barked an order, holding out his right hand. One of the warriors hurriedly put a whip in it: a heavy, thick, hardwood stock with a long lash of rhino hide.

Waziru snapped that lash. It made a cracking sound louder than the explosion of Hawkins' rifle.

"No Oparian has ever endured more than five strokes of this whip without crying out," Waziru said. "I am going to make you howl at its first cut!"

The whip slashed at Tarzan with all the power of Waziru's arm behind it.

Tarzan moved as that arm came down and forward. He leaped at Waziru, hand shooting up. It caught the lash in the air and pulled hard, jerking Waziru forward.

The Oparian chief screamed in rage, lifting the heavy wooden stock to use it as a club. Tarzan's hand shifted from lash to stock. For a space of brief seconds they struggled for

possession of it, chest to chest, Waziru's eyes now livid, his breath hot in Tarzan's face. Then Tarzan wrenched the stock from Waziru's grasp. He threw the whip into the river.

Waziru screamed again. He whipped both arms about Tarzan's body, squeezing hard, attempting to bend him backward, using ruthless pressure to break him.

Tremendous power surged in the man. He had not been chosen without good reason as chieftain of these savage warriors. And Tarzan was hampered in opposing him, for, as he had surmised, these Oparians oiled their bodies. It gave Waziru an advantage; trying to impose a grip of his own, Tarzan felt the man's skin slip beneath his hands.

And for a moment Waziru succeeded in his purpose. He forced Tarzan to bend backward, the only way he could relieve the intense strain against his spine and ribs. Waziru grunted in hard satisfaction. *"M-tu zanje,* you will squirm in the dirt, as I said!"

Tarzan called on all his strength. He used his hands on the Oparian chief, digging with fingers that clamped and held the flesh like steel pincers. And with that hold as leverage, he slowly straightened up, taking the bend out of his back. Then muscles bulged in his shoulders and legs.

Waziru had proposed to break him, make him grovel. Let the chief now taste the humiliation he had planned for Tarzan.

Mighty arms tightened about Waziru in a surge of irresistible power. It was Waziru whose back now was bent, who twisted and writhed helplessly in a grip he could not break. Bones creaked within him. A shuddering gasp was forced from his lips. His scarred face became purplish.

Tarzan abruptly let go. Waziru spilled down to the ground like an empty sack, and lay on his face. Tarzan put a foot against the back of his neck, holding him down.

The Oparian warriors stared at him with wondering eyes, too thunderstruck by this unbelievable happening to move. For a split second Tarzan returned their stares.

"Waziru struts like a peacock and brags like a baboon," he said contemptuously. "Look at him eating dirt! This will be the fate of all of you, if you do not at once return to Opar!"

They surged at him then, howling in wrath, spears lifted, arrows drawn back to the full tension of their bows.

Tarzan whirled. One long step and he leaped from the high bank, plummeting down to the river where the crocodiles waited.

Chapter 10 Hawkins Takes a Hand

Tarzan struck the water feet-first and went deep, so deep that his feet touched a silt bottom. He kicked strongly and shot toward the surface again.

But not all the way. The greatest peril to him was on the surface. His body curved. He swam on his back, eyes open. Sunlight filtered into the muddy water from above, enough of it to show him what was happening there.

The river was alive with the crocodiles surging toward him—churning stubby legs and flailing tails, jaws like steel traps, studded with razor-sharp teeth, that gaped wide to seize him and drag him to the bottom.

Tarzan dodged one and then another, buffeted by the currents set in motion by their furious charges. Then a monster among the great river lizards came driving at him from below. Tarzan sensed rather than saw it. He twisted

152

quickly away as it snapped at him. The beast's clamping jaws missed by inches. As they closed, Tarzan threw an arm about the crocodile's long, ugly snout, squeezing hard, holding those jaws closed.

In the same instant, he straddled the monster from beneath, gripping with his legs. Cold, scaly hide rasped his skin. He made this move to avoid the battering-ram sweep of its tail.

The crocodile writhed furiously, seeking to escape. Tarzan hung on. His knife was gripped in his right hand now. He shifted position, suddenly let go his hold on the beast, and simultaneously drew the knife in a long stroke up the only vulnerable spot it possessed—its soft under-belly. Then he shot away, swimming fast.

Still underwater, he swerved toward the river's far bank. He hugged the bottom. Crocodiles passed above him, swarming thickly. They paid him no heed.

At last Tarzan sought the surface, quickly gulping air in case he had to go under again.

But there was no need. He pulled himself up out of the water at the base of the east bank, some distance downstream from where he had gone into the river. There was no mud flat here, no crocodiles.

Out in the center of the river was a bellowing tumult, a ferocious champing of jaws. The crocodiles, cannibals all, no mercy in them for any creature, were tearing to pieces that one of their own kind that Tarzan had knifed.

Its blood-reek in the water had stirred them to frenzy. They had ignored him then, converging on that spot in the river as Tarzan had known they would; he had dealt with crocodiles before.

Across the channel, up on the island bank from which he had jumped, the Oparians were grouped, staring down at the boiling fury in the river below. One of them glimpsed Tarzan and shouted incredulously, pointing.

A deep-toned cry of fear and amazement sounded from all of them. They had seen the white man vanquish Waziru, had seen him plunge into the pool of crocodiles; now, miraculously, he had escaped from those rending jaws. Superstitious fear must be stirring in each of them.

Then Waziru appeared, with a bellow that silenced the others. The chieftain's face was contorted in rage. He seized a bow from one of the warriors and sent three arrows in whistling flight at Tarzan, hard-driven, with all the power in his massive shoulders behind them.

The distance was too great and the angle of fire too

acute; all of the arrows fell short.

Tarzan studied him grimly. He had not anticipated that his action in challenging Waziru, and besting him, would result in the chieftain being accorded the same treatment that he himself had brutally decreed for those two warriors left behind in the jungle. Waziru's harsh power over the Oparians was too great for that.

But the others would remember what had happened to Waziru. They would remember and perhaps be hesitant about risking an encounter with the man who could do such a thing to their chief. If this happened, the struggle with Waziru would have served a very good purpose.

Tarzan lifted his knife high, so that sunlight glittered brightly against its steel blade. It was both a gesture of defiance and of warning. The Oparians would remember that, too. Then Tarzan turned and went swiftly up the bank into the thick green cover at its top.

He worked northward, moving fast, hunting for the four who had seized Diana. They must still be on this side of the river, Tarzan told himself; they had reported to Waziru and would be waiting for further word from him.

This appraisal of the situation was confirmed presently

by the hollow thumps of rapid drum talk from the island. First, an order to those warriors still west of the river to come ahead fast, with a warning to avoid the mistake of crossing to the island. After that, orders for the four on this east bank where Tarzan hunted.

They were to hold the white woman, the message said, and hide with her. The white giant who ran through trees had appeared. His power was strong; he had escaped. The four were to avoid him. Waziru and his warriors would cross the channel from the island, but this would have to be done with care, for the crocodiles were swarming thickly. And the message being sent was not to be acknowledged.

Tarzan had to smile wryly at the last words. He had hoped for an acknowledgment, whose sound would guide him to where Diana was being held. But Waziru, in spite of his rage, was being canny; he had taken into account that Tarzan would be listening.

His eagerness to seize Tarzan again would be driving Waziru hard. Still, it would take some little time for the chieftain and his warriors to get across the channel.

It was too deep for them to ford, judging by the depth Tarzan had found when he plunged among the crocodiles. It was not likely that they had much skill at swimming, since they were mountain people.

They would have to cross over on logs, straddling them, yelling and beating the water to keep the crocodiles away, probably the same way they had reached the island. And as soon as they had acquired the necessary logs, it would be done quickly. Tarzan had to find Diana before they came up the bank on this side.

He moved even more quickly, working back and forth through the undergrowth and among the trees, every faculty sharply alert for anything that would guide him to Diana's captors. But Tarzan encountered no sound or scent that was helpful.

Then, after about half an hour of this hurried searching, he suddenly heard another drum message—but one that he did not understand at all.

It sounded more like a rapid clicking than somebody beating against a hollow log, a quick combination of long and short taps, five of them in all. After a moment of silence, it was repeated. Tarzan counted them—two shorts, one long, then a short and a long. And the location of the sounds baffled him because of their strange character and the quickness with which they were made. He could not tell whether they came from the island or whether they were on this side of the river channel.

Silence again. The sun was now high and hot. Then Tarzan heard a crashing in the junglelike tangles along the bank, somebody or something plunging at a reckless, heedless pace toward him.

He put a hand quickly on his knife, frowning as he sought a meaning for this. A moment later scent told him who it was, and his frown deepened. Tarzan went forward, leaped from cover, and clamped his hand on the arm of the man who was plunging along, making more noise than a buffalo on a rampage.

"Hold up, Penrod!" Tarzan's voice was vibrant with exasperation. "Confound it, why didn't you stay at the lake, as I ordered? The noise you've been making must have been heard by everybody within two miles of here!"

Dick Penrod's face was white and lined. He shook off Tarzan's hand with a furious sweep of his arm. "How could I stay there with Diana in danger? And—" his fists knotted convulsively "—I hope I was heard! I want them to jump me, too—want a chance to get my hands on them!"

"You'll likely get that chance," Tarzan told him grimly. "I've been trying to locate the four who grabbed your wife, with precious little time in which to do it. The noise you made has warned them; you've ruined any opportunity I might have had to find her. There are twelve like the four who seized Diana, just beyond the river yonder, who'll soon be here. And there are even more on the way. If it's fighting you want, you'll get plenty of that. But you won't be helping Diana any, and you'll be captured yourself. That's what you've accomplished by disobeying my order!"

Penrod rubbed his face. "I'm sorry," he said quietly. "But I'd do the same thing if it happened again."

Tarzan grunted at this. It was exactly as he had said; Penrod's reckless move had accomplished nothing. And yet the man had to be admired for having made it.

"Listen, Tarzan," Penrod went on, "I know you're right. But I want to be with her, even if we're both captives. And there's no sense in your being grabbed, also. You've done all you could for us—more, probably, than we're worth. Leave me while you can. Turn back. Save the others if that's possible—"

A sudden barbarous, rhythmic chanting came from the river. Waziru and the warriors with him were beginning to move across the channel between that island and this east bank.

Tarzan said, "I'll save all of you or none. Those others

are heading this way. Come with me. We may be able to fight them off, keep them from getting ashore."

He knew it was a forlorn hope at best. They could grapple with the first warriors to climb the steep bank, perhaps throw several of them into the river—though there would be the danger that he and Penrod would go into it, too.

But the others would swarm quickly up from the channel. Two against twelve, with the probability that those four holding Diana would also emerge from hiding to lend a hand! The chance of accomplishing anything seemed very slim. However, it had to be taken. There was no other move that could be made now.

Penrod grinned eagerly, lifting his clenched fists. "I'm right with you, Tarzan! Lead me to them!"

Tarzan turned toward the river. He took three strides and stopped, brow wrinkling in surprise.

A sudden chattering had begun, Oparians talking excitedly together off to northward, along with a crackling of brush. Then a yell: "Waziru! *Im tumbi langa!*"

"Waziru! We have a message for you!" That was the meaning of those words.

What message? They must be the ones who had seized

Diana. Why had they broken silence, revealed their location?

Tarzan swerved toward the sound of those voices. Penrod was at his heels. But again he had taken only several steps when another shout sounded, this time from off to the right, eastward:

"Tarzan! Come here, quick!"

It was the voice of Josiah Hawkins, who had slipped far to the back of Tarzan's thoughts. He was now nearby; he had also left the lake.

Then Hawkins yelled again, "I've got Mrs. Penrod!"

Dick cried out at that, starting to thrust past Tarzan, who put out an arm to stop him.

"No," Tarzan said. "There'll be no more reckless rushing about!"

"But he rescued Diana! I want to go to her!"

"It may be a trap, with one of those warriors holding a spear against his throat, as with Camage Dean," Tarzan said. "You wait until I have a lead of about ten feet, then follow me."

The chanting from the river had increased in volume. Tarzan moved in a hurry, Penrod trailing him.

Tarzan came to edge of the junglelike growth that

fringed the river. He looked ahead, then lifted his hand, a sharp warning for Penrod to stop.

Hawkins was out in the open, yonder. He had an arm about Diana Penrod, supporting her, and was facing toward the south. He called again, "Tarzan!"

A gesture for Penrod to come on, then Tarzan began to run.

Hawkins' head turned. He grimaced. "Been scared stiff you wouldn't show up!" He squinted at Penrod, who had now appeared, also. "What in blazes is he doing here?"

"Never mind that, Hawkins." Diana was sagging in Hawkins' embrace, semiconscious if that much, her eyes open and her lips moving fearfully. She did not seem to know where she was or to have any awareness of what was going on. Tarzan continued, "How did you manage to rescue her?"

"Oh, nothing much to that," Hawkins answered. "When you took off after those who grabbed her, there near the lake, I figured right away you were going at it wrong. There was only one direction for them to head, and that was toward the river, yonder. I cut around the cliff where we made camp and took a short cut, planning to head them off—"

Penrod joined them, panting hard from his exertions. Hawkins turned Diana over to him. Penrod spoke soothingly to his wife. She stared at him, blank-eyed, and moaned.

Hawkins was breathing fairly hard, also. Tarzan said, "Tell the rest of it. Hurry up!"

"Why, nothing much more to tell," Hawkins said. "They went into cover, north of here a piece, and beat out a message on a log—that they had grabbed Mrs. Penrod, I guess. I couldn't spot them from that, though. Knew I had to do it quick, so used my head. Saw a thick stand of thornbush, and felt it was pretty certain that's where they were hiding. So I yelled that I was going to empty my rifle into it. They popped out the other side like rabbits running from a lion dog. I went into the thornbush and found Mrs. Penrod, came out and started calling for you."

The thornbush was visible off to the north, a gray plant, or rather a grouping of many plants, about head-high, covering a considerable area and matted very thickly.

Tarzan noticed a swelling above Diana's right temple, at the hairline. She had been hit, probably with a spear shaft, to knock her out and silence her when she screamed that one time, he thought.

He said, "Hawkins, were you bluffing or did you load your rifle?"

For answer, the lanky man worked his rifle's ejector, showing the magazine was empty. "Moved too quick to load it. Sure, I was bluffing! You don't think I'd have fired, with the danger of hitting Mrs. Penrod, do you?" Then, nervously, "We'd better get away from here. I don't know who's making that racket over at the river, or why, but it doesn't mean anything good for us!"

Tarzan nodded in agreement. Penrod was trying to help Diana walk, but it was obvious she was still too unsteady for that. Tarzan said, "Let me," and lifted her. "Penrod, go ahead, back toward the lake. Hawkins, follow along. This time you may have to use your rifle."

"Don't worry; I will!" Hawkins said. "Just get moving!"

Tarzan started at a quick trot, Diana cradled in his arms, with Penrod running ahead of him. They dodged through the thin, veldtlike stretch of timber where he had tracked the four Oparians earlier. It seemed hours had elapsed since then, though Tarzan knew much less time had passed.

And as he ran, knowing the peril had not been diminished, that pursuit by Waziru would be swift and vengeful,

with no plan yet for how it might be avoided, Tarzan gave some thought to the story Hawkins had told.

A very odd story, indeed, he told himself. He simply did not believe Diana had been rescued the way Hawkins had described, with a convenient guess on his part that the Oparians were hiding in a clump of thornbush, followed by their panicky flight when he threatened to rake it with fire from his light rifle.

Tarzan had not heard Hawkins make any such threat; he felt certain it had not been made at all. The lanky man had done something else that had persuaded the Oparians to let Diana go.

But digging for the true story of what had happened could wait until later. Right now the important thing was that Diana had been rescued, and never mind how.

And there could be no doubt that Hawkins' attitude had undergone a radical change. He was extremely eager to get away from this neighborhood as fast as possible. He pounded along, close behind Tarzan, begging him to run even faster.

An urgent signal to Camage and Fletcher brought those two along to join them, when they emerged from the trees near the lake. Camage, helped by Chetah, carried the supplies, including the bindles Tarzan had made earlier, though he noticed that his coil of vine-rope had been left behind.

Fletcher carried nothing. He expressed great concern for Diana, together with a blustering threat: "If I ever get my hands on those who grabbed her—"

"Forget that," Tarzan told him shortly. "Penrod, lead out again. On southward."

It was the only way open to them. The Oparians barred escape to westward. North, there was only vast emptiness, all the way to the Sudan. Eastward, the lake lay squarely in their way, and, beyond the lake, that barren country lifting toward the mountains of Ethiopia.

To the south were those low hills, and a possibility of shaking off the pursuers among them, though it seemed probable the veldt lay just beyond. However, the risk had to be taken that they would be driven out onto the veldt and caught there.

Diana could now stand and walk alone, though she was still wobbly. She could not remember anything that had happened since the moment the four Oparians had seized her, neither Hawkins' rescue nor Tarzan carrying her; it was only at the lake that her senses began to return.

Camage put an arm about Diana, and the two women hurried along together. Fletcher was closely following Penrod. Tarzan and Hawkins brought up the rear.

Chetah scrambled beside Tarzan, who was carrying the supplies. She scolded him for leaving the camp so fast a while ago that she could not accompany him. Then she suddenly bounced ahead, out in front of Penrod, the small bindle thrust over her shoulder, heading for some trees clustered near the water's edge. She disappeared among them.

Shouting began behind them, though a glance in that direction showed the Oparians had not yet appeared.

"We've got about a two-mile lead, I figure, but they're coming after us fast," Hawkins muttered. "Tarzan, nothing much ahead of us but to reach those hills. Then we'd better look for some place to stop, a nest of boulders, maybe, where we'll have some protection, and try to fight them off."

Tarzan shook his head. To stop would be fatal. They could hold off the Oparians for a while, until Hawkins' supply of cartridges was exhausted. Then they would be overwhelmed. They had to keep running.

Then Camage Dean stumbled and fell, heavily. She

struggled up again and went on, limping, at a much slower pace, mouth tight with anguish; Camage had painfully wrenched her ankle in that fall.

Diana wavered along beside her.

The shouting from behind grew louder. Tarzan's mouth tightened grimly. Neither of the women could last much longer. Unless something unforeseen happened at once, they were sure to fall into the Oparians' hands.

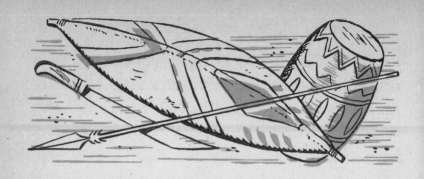

Chapter 11   A Long Chance

Chetah suddenly reappeared at the edge of a grove of rather large willowlike trees clustered thickly at the extreme south end of the lake. She waved an arm excitedly, calling to Tarzan to hurry.

She had found something yonder. Tarzan ran past the others, in among the trees. What he saw made him stop short with an instant stir of hope.

He had given no particular thought before as to how this lake was formed and fed—by streams off to northward, he supposed—or how it was drained, but the answer to the latter question was now before him, a sizable stream flowing out of the lake toward the south.

And it was no sluggish, muddy river like that other one off to the west, but a brawling, foaming current that rushed off at a fast pace, whipping around a bend half a mile away. The land obviously dipped downward—or, rather, the whole country lifted on a long slant toward those Ethiopian mountains. Thus, this stream that flowed south and east dropped down a long incline, with a very fast rate of fall.

Also, it had gouged out a fairly deep canyon among the low brown hills, with walls almost as sheer as those of the gorge where the plane had crashed.

Tarzan studied the river for a moment, turning these factors over in his head. Then he began to cast back and forth in the grove, studying the downed timber there: the old trees that had fallen, the younger ones that were also on the ground. There were a number of both.

The others came along to join him. Dick Penrod stared at the river and wearily shook his head. It was only about a dozen yards wide where it began, but water spilled from the lake there at a race-horse pace. "We're stymied," he said. "We can't get across that."

Hawkins wasted no time in studying the river. He had known at once what Tarzan was seeking, and began to search about in the grove also. "Over here!" he called.

Tarzan shook his head. "I saw that log. It's too big. We need something smaller."

"But this one is plenty big enough to carry all of us," Hawkins objected.

"We're going to split up," Tarzan said. "I've a feeling a log with more than three people on it is liable to founder in that current."

A moment later he found one of the logs he sought, a tree just past sapling size that had been downed, its roots washed out of the soil perhaps during the last big rains. Tarzan used his knife, slashing off dead branches. "All of you, lend a hand here!"

Fletcher stared at him. "You're planning to put that thing in the river and expect us to ride it? But it can't be done! We'll all be drowned or have our necks broken!"

"Stay here if you'd rather!" Hawkins growled.

Fletcher reluctantly helped in the arduous business of pushing and shoving at the log until it was at the edge of the brawling stream. Chetah lent a hand, too, tugging at the nubbin where a branch had been, chirping in excitement.

They turned back then, found another one, and got it to the stream also; with minutes swiftly passing, the pressure of time bore heavily on all of them. That distant shouting continued, partially dimmed by the tumult made by the little river as it rushed down its narrow canyon.

"Hawkins, you'll go first, with Fletcher and Miss Dean," Tarzan said. "Safeguard that rifle."

"Yeah." The lanky man shoved its barrel under his belt so that the weapon was crosswise across his body. "Guess I'd better ride the front of the log, and fend it away from rocks, or the bank. I'll need a pole for that. Fletcher, you get one, too."

They worked the log hurriedly into the current. Tarzan, water boiling about his waist, held it steady. "Get on first, Miss Dean, at the middle. You'll have to straddle it, and grip hard with your knees."

Camage obeyed him. Fletcher gingerly climbed on at the rear of the log, gripping the long branch he had picked up. Hawkins then settled himself at the front. He had a pole, also.

"Keep the log heading straight," Tarzan warned. "If it swings sideways the current is liable to roll it over and throw all of you off."

"I know," Hawkins growled. "Rode about forty miles of the upper Congo rapids this way once, running from pygmy head-hunters." He twisted to look back. "Fletcher, you keep your pole working!"

Tarzan said, "Penrod, bring two of those bindles I fixed —also, one of the water flasks."

He gave one of the bindles to Camage Dean. "Hold on tight to this," Tarzan told her.

She nodded steadily. "I will."

He put the flask in the other one and passed it to Fletcher. "Put the stick through your belt, as Hawkins did with his rifle. It doesn't seem likely we'll be separated, since our log will be right behind yours. But if that should happen, you have several days' rations in the bindles. Make them last as long as possible—"

Dick Penrod said tautly, "Tarzan, you'd better hurry it up. That yelling is getting pretty loud."

Tarzan was hearing it, also. "Good luck!" he said, and gave the log a shove.

It seemed to move slowly at first, close to the bank. Hawkins gave a hard shove with his pole, forcing the strange craft into the full grip of the current. Then it suddenly leaped forward, its front end surging above the surface for a moment, falling back. It raced toward the bend in the canyon at dizzying speed.

Tarzan turned to the other log. "Mrs. Penrod, get on quickly, please."

She was chewing her lip. "I—I don't think I can!"

"Diana, you must!" Penrod took her arm, pushing her at the log which Tarzan was holding steady in the river.

Diana slapped at his hands, near hysteria again. It took several precious minutes for her husband to get her on the log, to hand her the bindles to hold. Tarzan, meanwhile, had fastened the coat-wrapped bundle securely to a protruding stub.

Penrod hurried to the log's far end. He had found a pole for himself, a springy branch ripped from one of the trees and its foliage torn off. Tarzan had one like it.

"Ready!" Penrod called.

And now, at this last moment when it appeared they would get away from this place unhindered, they found that one of their party did not intend to go along.

Chetah sat on the bank, bindle-stick over her shoulder and gripped in one hand. She had watched the business of floating the logs with obvious uneasiness, had jumped about in chattering protest when the first one had raced away downstream.

Tarzan said, "Little one, come here. Hurry!"

Chetah huddled and stared at the ground. Her lips were thrust out mutinously. She muttered something in an angry tone, and beat her free hand against the earth.

This development was something Chetah had not counted on when she had hurried ahead, found the river, and turned back to report it. She had felt certain Tarzan would make some use of it, but not that he would do such a mad thing as this—to trust himself to a slippery log in that foaming, treacherous, and very wet current.

That he should expect her to go along was too much. Chetah hated getting wet as much as she hated baboons. She reminded Tarzan of this, voice rising. She would not trust herself to that log—not ever. She would stay right where she was, rather than do such a thing.

Penrod said, voice cracking with strain, "Those natives are almost here!"

"I haven't the time to argue with you," Tarzan told Chetah. "Come along now—at once. This is your last chance!"

Chetah blew through her lips and pretended she hadn't heard him.

Tarzan pushed the log out into the full current of the brawling stream that poured from the lake. He swung himself on it at the front end, gripping with his legs, shoving with his pole to give it even more momentum. It began to move swiftly away from the bank and Chetah.

This was something that wrenched him inwardly, a thing he had never guessed that he would be forced to do. But the welfare of one small, very stubborn chimpanzee, balanced against the lives of five humans—it was the only thing he could do.

Chetah squealed in unbelieving dismay. Then she was running along the bank, faster than she had ever run before. A prodigious leap carried her to the log. She landed in front of Tarzan, slipped, and almost went into the river. He hauled her up, feet and legs dripping, yelping in fright and anger. Chetah squirmed and twisted, shaking herself like a cat, and began making shrill protests at having been nearly left behind, at being wet, at this whole insane venture.

"Hush up," Tarzan said. "Sit down in front of me as close as you can get, and stay still."

Ahead of them the log bearing the other three was being whipped by the current around that narrow bend. Tarzan twisted to look back. No one showed yet among the trees that were dropping swiftly behind them.

Diana Penrod was bent forward, both arms about the log, clinging desperately. He could not see her face. Dick

Penrod, jaw set, had his pole raised, ready for instant use.

Tarzan faced forward again. The log was moving swiftly, smoothly, showing no tendency yet to roll or swing sideways against the current. The walls of the canyon gouged out by this nameless little river sloped up on either side, barren and bleak, colored red and brown and black, with the sky a narrow lane of blue directly overhead.

That canyon could be a deadly trap. Occasional small, narrow beaches showed on either side, brief stretches of sand where they might possibly struggle ashore if the log rolled over and threw them off, but the canyon walls were too steep and smooth for even Tarzan to scale.

Tarzan noted these things, the possibilities for disaster, with an inward resolution to avoid them, as the log bore down at increasing speed on the bend already traversed by Hawkins and the others.

A call from Penrod; he looked back, to see an Oparian at the spot on the river bank they had left moments ago— then another, with more pouring through the trees to cluster there.

Tarzan had hoped to be around the bend before they arrived, to gain a little time before the Oparians realized where their quarry had gone. That had not happened. And what they were doing, Waziru and his warriors could do, also.

Tarzan shrugged off this thought. He had other things to worry about besides further pursuit. He gestured urgently to Penrod, pointing toward the bend which they were fast approaching. Penrod nodded understandingly, pole lifted and ready.

As the log went into the bend, it was forced sideways by the driving force of the current, and sheered dangerously close to a canyon wall. Tarzan thrust hard against rock with his pole. Penrod did the same. Working together, they made it around the bend, and were flying downstream again.

But another bend was ahead of them, and then, immediately, another. They made those two turns successfully, also. Far ahead, down a long, straight stretch, Tarzan had a momentary glimpse of the other log, before it vanished around still another twist in the canyon.

Chetah had forgotten her first fright. This swift, smooth way of travel delighted her. She stirred and stood up, begging that she be allowed to hold and wave Tarzan's pole.

With no warning, they were suddenly in rough water, waves piled up by hidden rocks or ledges. The log was slammed joltingly back and forth in the narrow channel. Blinding sheets of spray hit and drenched them.

Chetah cried out in new fear, turning and clinging to Tarzan, begging frantically for him to stop the log so she could get off.

He had no time to devote to her, no time for anything other than swift, lightninglike thrusts of his pole, first on one side and then the other, fending this frail and uncertain craft away from rocks that he could see, while praying that some invisible, submerged chunk of granite would not smash against it and hurl all of them into the river.

Penrod was furiously busy, also. Miraculously, they made it through that stretch of turbulent water and were flying along smoothly again. Chetah was silent, still huddled against Tarzan. She was thoroughly wet now, and miserable.

Another call from Penrod. Tarzan looked back and saw a dot on the water behind them, just entering the long channel. It was another log, with four Oparians riding it —no, five. Tarzan shook his head as he counted them.

He continued to watch, between quick surveys of the river ahead, until the following log plunged into the rough water, and felt no great surprise when he saw its forward

end suddenly tilt high, as it slewed violently sideways. Then it was being thrown this way and that among submerged rocks, no longer guided. All who had been riding it had been shaken into the river.

It had been dangerously overloaded. And if Waziru continued to make the same mistake, as he sent the rest of his warriors downstream, perhaps the danger from them was now definitely past.

But the danger from the river was not. They traversed more narrow, twisting bends, rode through another area of rough water, and encountered a brief stretch of violent rapids. Then on again, with no further sight of those who went before them.

Time passed—how much, Tarzan did not know, though he had a sense of minutes and then hours ticking away. It was a curious thing that he had noticed before: in moments of stress and action, time seemed to telescope, to melt away much more rapidly than when one was sitting idly, doing nothing. Morning of this day was now behind them. They were well into the afternoon.

After a while he saw that the current of the river was definitely moderating. The canyon walls were moving back from it and flattening out.

There were some changes that Tarzan did not like: mud-banks appearing, the river channel widening, with lesser channels beginning to thread their way off on either side, sluggish streams winding through hummocks of saw grass, past gaunt trees that trailed streamers of moss like tattered shawls.

At the first of those branching channels Tarzan hesitated, half-impelled to turn aside. But he shook his head. Hawkins, he thought, would not have left the main stream.

He let the log drift on, with a deepening concern as signs increased as to where they were now, until there were too many of them to be denied. Crocodile tracks on the banks, masses of brilliant water lilies like floating rafts, squawking waterfowl, more and more channels forking away in all directions until it was now difficult to determine where the main channel was—and those trees, the hummocks of saw grass, stagnant pools. It all added up to only one thing. They were in a swamp of unknown size.

The river had ended its tumultuous rush down from that blue lake in a depression from which it could not escape. Perhaps the muddy river off to westward emptied into it, also.

Swamps were all too common in Africa, but Tarzan

had not anticipated that today's wild journey would end in one. It was a fact that now had to be accepted, with plans to be made for getting out of it again.

More worrisome than that was another fact: they had lost the other three members of their party, with no sign to indicate where they had gone, no way of knowing whether they were still ahead of them or had turned, by plan or mistake, into one of the many branching channels.

Tarzan kept hoping they would find the others, until the time arrived when the current had slowed until the log was scarcely moving at all.

Then he spoke over his shoulder: "This is as far as we can go. We'll have to land."

Dick Penrod said, "You think we've passed Hawkins, Camage, and Fletcher, that they're somewhere behind us?"

"I think that now, yes," Tarzan said.

Then he filled his lungs with air and sent a mighty shout through the swamp: "Hello! Hawkins!"

Only the echoes of his voice came back as he listened intently.

He shouted again, and still a third time. There was no answer.

Tarzan studied the stretch of water between the raft

and the nearest land. Several ripples showed in the lazy
current.

He pointed to the ripples. "Those are crocodiles. Keep
an eye on them and warn me if they come any closer."

He slid into the water and began to swim, towing the
log. The crocodiles kept their distance.

Tarzan beached the log against a hummock of spongy
land. Their river journey was over.

Chapter 12   The Swamp

Chetah was the first one ashore, bounding from log to land, running for a tree and climbing it—a swamp mangrove with a fantastic spread of roots above the ground. She perched on a limb, still wet and bedraggled, her bindle slanted over one shoulder, and muttered angrily to herself about the indignities that she had been forced to endure.

Tarzan and Penrod helped Diana ashore. Diana's clothing was sodden, and her face and arms had been blistered by the action of water and sun. Her hair was an unkempt tangle. She had lost her shoes.

But she refused to yield to the deep weariness she must be feeling, and Tarzan noted with approval that she still had the two bindles which had been handed her at the lake; she had clung to them all during that wild rush down the turbulent stream.

"I'm all right," she said. "Don't fuss over me!"

Tarzan took a quick look around. This hummock thrust above the water a few feet, like many others in sight; they were separated by channels and stagnant pools. Moss-shrouded mangroves grew thickly, with much rank plant growth about their bases. The hummocks, like this one, were covered by high, brownish saw grass. Many stretches of water were choked by the mats of swamp lilies, with spearlike reeds along their margins.

It was a place, Tarzan knew, with many kinds of animal life, some very dangerous. He beat through the grass with care, and some small furry creatures fled squeaking before him. Tarzan noted their presence and turned back.

Diana was clawing distractedly at her hair. "I must look like a witch!" she said.

Tarzan went for the coat-wrapped bundle. He delved in it for one of the items he had picked up at the plane, forgotten until now because of the rush of events that had driven it from his thoughts.

He held it out to Diana, Camage Dean's bag. "Perhaps you can find something in this that will help."

Diana's hands trembled as she pulled it open, and she cried out joyfully: "There's a comb! And a small jar of cold cream! And a bottle of cologne!"

Tarzan and Dick Penrod exchanged smiles as she bent in absorption over those treasures.

"Let's get a fire started," Tarzan said.

"We'll spend the night here?" Penrod asked.

"Perhaps." He didn't know yet. It depended on a great many things. Hawkins and those with him might be along to join them, so they should wait. But Waziru and his warriors might work this far down the river channel, also, and they might have to run.

With full night, they sat beside the fire. A pale moon was rising. Crocodiles bellowed occasionally. Far off, a lion coughed—and since Numa was never to be found in swampland, this indicated the watery wilderness was not very large in extent; they could soon find their way out of it.

Chetah was still in the mangrove, aloofly refusing to come down. Diana was combing her hair, taking great pleasure in that simple act.

Dick Penrod said, "I don't know what we had for dinner, but it was delicious. What sort of animal was it anyway?"

"A kind of ground squirrel," Tarzan answered. It was

actually cane rat, and quite good eating, but there was no need to give its true name. Tarzan had gone back to where he had seen those small furry creatures, had used a make-shift club to tap the ground near burrow openings, then had nabbed the animals when their heads inquisitively appeared.

Four of their carcasses were still browning—for tomorrow's breakfast, or for Hawkins, Camage, and Fletcher, should they appear. Another tin of the English biscuits had added to the meal, with a chocolate bar for dessert.

"Keep the fire burning," Tarzan said, rising. He had rigged Diana's coat to hide its glow from the channel along which they had approached this spot. Perhaps an unneces-sary precaution, with night now here. The Oparians might be in the swamp, but they would remain where they were until dawn.

Diana said, "Are we just going to take it easy here? I'm thinking of poor Hal—this terrible experience is so hard for him to bear. And Camage; she's such a coward, always afraid of her own shadow—"

Penrod shifted position uncomfortably. "Diana, what can we do? They might be anywhere in this swamp; we can't look for them in the dark!"

His wife sniffed angrily. "I don't expect *you* to do anything," she said. "You hung back when those four awful men seized me this morning. It was Hawkins who came to rescue me; he told me so, there at the grove of trees just before he left us."

Her hectoring made Tarzan uncomfortable. He left them and went to the mangrove. It was an old tree, almost at the end of its life cycle, with a hollowed-out trunk. Tarzan tapped it experimentally with the club he had picked up, and produced a booming sound.

Chetah stirred above him. She complained peevishly about that racket.

"Why don't you come down from there?" Tarzan said. "I didn't scare you and get you wet on purpose. It couldn't be avoided."

Chetah snorted at this and began an angry, chattering speech. It was all Tarzan's fault, everything that had happened, beginning when they had joined those helpless humans. It had brought them to this swamp, which she didn't like at all. Chetah was wet and cold and hungry. She sneezed, a doleful sound.

"It's warm and comfortable by the fire," Tarzan said. "I can give you a biscuit to chew on, also a piece of sweet chocolate."

Chetah whimpered hungrily at this, greatly tempted by the promise of chocolate. But she still refused to come down.

"Be stubborn and stay where you are then," Tarzan said, and began to beat against the mangrove trunk.

He sent out the quick double roll, three times repeated, that was the questioning call. It asked anyone who heard it to reply.

It was a sound that should be audible much farther than his previous inquiring shouts. Hawkins had admitted some knowledge of drum talk, and should know the questioning call. He could make an answer that would indicate where he and the others were—could trigger his rifle, if nothing else.

But no answer came, though Tarzan sent out the call again and again. The trunk-drumming fretted a number of crocodiles, who bellowed and slapped the water with their tails in the nearby river channel.

Tarzan presently returned to the fire. Dick Penrod was not there. He had gone to stand at the edge of the channel.

"Dick has an idea one of those creatures might try to join us here," Diana said. "I don't know what he would do if that happened. Nothing, probably, just as he did this morning."

Tarzan studied her thoughtfully for a moment, then dropped to one knee beside Diana Penrod. He told her, low-voiced, of the bravery Dick Penrod had displayed this morning, of his deep anxiety for her.

And then he went on to join Penrod, leaving Diana with a strained, startled expression on her face. Perhaps she was reviewing and regretting her recent behavior—and many things, as well, that she had done before she had ever seen Africa.

Penrod reported, "Those creatures are doing a lot of bellowing, but they don't seem inclined to leave the water."

"Crocs have a deep fear of fire," Tarzan said. "They won't bother us as long as we keep it burning."

"Oh," Penrod said. Then, "I heard you signaling. There was no reply?"

Tarzan shook his head. The other man went on, "I wish there had been—can't feel too much concern for Hawkins and Fletcher, but I'm worried about Camage. Wherever she is, it must be pretty rough on her. Camage is completely dependent on Diana, and frightens so easily."

He must not have noticed, Tarzan thought, that there had been a considerable change in Camage Dean these past two days.

"I'll watch the channel for a while," Tarzan said. "You go and tend the fire."

"All right. . . . About those natives following us—do you think we've managed to lose them?"

"I hope so," Tarzan said.

Penrod started to turn away, but paused for an instant. "You know what I've been thinking? All the ground we've covered, yesterday and today, with so much effort—we could have traveled the same distance in a plane in about ten minutes."

"Probably less," Tarzan said. And, "You like flying?"

"Yes," Penrod answered. "I meant to make a career of it in the Navy. But—well, it didn't work out. Diana wanted to travel after we were married, and I couldn't manage that and stay in the Navy. So I resigned my commission."

He left then, to return to the fire. Tarzan began to watch the river channel.

But not for long. It had been a settled fact in his mind that if there was no sign from the others by a certain time, he had to go out into the swamp and search for them. That time was now here.

He skirted around the fire where the Penrods sat silently, across from each other, and then headed swiftly toward the north end of the hummock.

Tarzan paused there, at the margin of a shallow pool. He studied the moonlit morass northward, listening hard.

Chetah suddenly stirred on her limb, then squeaked excitedly, came down with a rush, and ran to join him. She jumped up and down, pointing out into the night.

"I heard it," Tarzan said. "Keep quiet for a moment."

Both of them heard it again, the hoarse yell of a man.

It was a thin, distant sound. Tarzan marked its direction and plunged into the shallow pool, wading toward another hummock beyond. Chetah cried out in protest. She wanted to go along.

"Stay back!" Tarzan ordered over his shoulder. "There may be a python or a crocodile out there with its mouth wide open, just waiting for you!"

He worked swiftly through the swamp, fording more pools and channels, forcing his way through the masses of thick reeds, taking to trees when they were available. Various rustlings, growls, and scurrying sounds came from swamp creatures that he disturbed.

Again that yell, and this time Tarzan recognized the man's voice. It was Hal Fletcher. Tarzan called back, "Work toward me!"

Fletcher was north and east of him. They met a good mile or more from where he had left Chetah. Fletcher was stumbling noisily along, with a loud splashing; he fell into a fairly deep pool just as Tarzan reached him, and floundered about there. Tarzan jumped in and pulled him out.

The man was wheezing hard. He was hoarse from much yelling. "You sure took your time about coming to help me," he muttered ungraciously.

Tarzan gripped his arm. "Where are Hawkins and Miss Dean?" he demanded.

"Oh, Hawkins went wandering off sometime before sunset. Said he'd hunt for you, but then he didn't come back," Fletcher reported. "Maybe something happened to him. I decided I wasn't going to just sit there, especially as I got the feeling that those devils who grabbed Diana were somewhere close—"

"Why? Did you see or hear them?"

"Well, no. But we got down the river, so they must have done it, too, and I wasn't going to stay there and wait for them! I started to hunt for you on my own."

Tarzan said, "What about Miss Dean?"

"She's all right. Would have held me up because of her bad ankle, so I left her somewhere yonder—" Fletcher gestured vaguely in a northeasterly direction. "I said you'd come get her, soon as I located you. Listen, where's your camp? I'm starved; that food you gave us didn't make more than a couple of mouthfuls."

Tarzan pointed. "That way. A mile or so. Keep going."

"Huh? Aren't you going to come along, help me get there?"

"Fletcher, you have two choices—wait here until I come back, or find it by yourself," Tarzan said. "And I don't care which one you choose!"

He left then, going to search for Camage Dean, moving fast as he thought of her alone in this swamp by night. Tarzan spent no time being angry with Hal Fletcher. Anger would be wasted on him. It was completely in keeping with the man's character that he had gone off and left Camage alone.

Fletcher had feared the Oparians, but had felt no compunction at leaving Camage to them, should they find the place where Hawkins had stopped.

For Hawkins to leave the two of them, completely inexperienced as they were at surviving in a swamp, was even worse. He should have taken Fletcher and Camage with him, or stayed and waited for a signal from Tarzan, instead of trying to locate him . . . if that was what Hawkins had attempted to do. It seemed unlikely that he had. If Hawkins had made such a search, it would have been successful by this time.

But the explanation of Hawkins' conduct could wait until later. Right now Tarzan began to call Camage's name, working back and forth along a line in the direction Hal Fletcher had indicated.

It seemed a long while before he heard her voice. Tarzan moved quickly toward the sound of it, saw the ruddy glow of a fire, and discovered Camage Dean on a hummock like the one he had left.

Judging distances in a swamp by night was difficult, but Tarzan thought the place was at least five miles from the other camp, and nearly as far from the river channel.

Camage greeted him with a strained smile. "I'm so glad you're here. There have been some rather frightening noises, and things prowling close to the fire. I could see the shine of their eyes."

She had been in some danger here. There were creatures of the swamp that did not share the crocodiles' fear of fire: the dull brain of the python, for instance, did not understand fear at all. And a smaller cousin of the jungle leopard made its home in this sort of morass. Tarzan had heard the hunting scream of one some moments ago.

Camage's manner was steady and quiet, though, like Diana, she had suffered from the ordeal she had undergone yesterday and today. Her clothing was dry, but badly tattered, and fitted her loosely; Camage had lost some of her plumpness. Her hair, of finer texture and a lighter shade of brown than Diana's, hung in limp, matted strands. She had been scorched by the sun, and her lips were blistered.

Camage said, "Diana and Dick—they're all right?"

"Yes," Tarzan said. "And Fletcher, also—at least, he was when I ran into him."

"I didn't like to be left alone, but there was nothing I could do to stop him," Camage said. "Besides, if he had stayed and something had happened, Hal's first concern would have been for himself, not for me."

Camage, Tarzan thought, was learning much from the things that were happening to her.

"I—I used to admire him," she went on. "It's only in the past two days that I've come to understand the sort of person he really is."

Tarzan began to put out the fire. The Oparians might be in the swamp and they might find this spot in the morning, but he did not mean to mark its location for them tonight, if that could be avoided. He asked, "How did it happen that Hawkins brought you to this particular place?"

"Well, he said we had to get away from the main river channel, in case you didn't manage to make it down the canyon but those people who seized Diana did. So he turned the log into one of the side channels and finally stopped here. He made a fire and we had a meal—from my bindle. Hal lost his, coming down the river. Then Hawkins said he would look for you and went away."

So Hawkins must have been gone about three hours, more than enough time to locate Tarzan's group if that had been his purpose.

"We can't wait for him," Tarzan said. "Can you walk at all?"

"Oh, yes—though slowly." Camage took a few steps to demonstrate, limping on the ankle she had injured.

Tarzan picked up her bindle and tore the cloth comprising it into strips, then knelt to wind them in a tight bandage about the ankle. "I could carry you," he said, "but you must work out the soreness as soon as possible. Walk back and forth for a moment."

He busied himself making signs for Hawkins: an arrow

scratched in moist dirt, pointing toward the southeast, a blade of saw grass bent in the same direction, a slash on a mangrove trunk. Signs that might also guide the Oparians, but that had to be risked.

They started out then, working from hummock to hummock at a slow pace—had gone perhaps half a mile when Tarzan suddenly touched Camage's arm. "Wait a minute!" he breathed.

A distant sound in the night—drumbeats. And he was hearing again that five-beat message he had heard this morning: two short, one long, a short and a long.

This time it was answered, from even farther away, a swift flurry of taps that conveyed no meaning.

Beyond those two quick bursts of sound there was nothing more.

Camage whispered, "What does it mean?"

"I don't know," Tarzan answered.

And, in a literal sense, he did not. But the mere fact that the sounds had been made apprised him of one very disquieting certainty.

Some of the Oparians had made it down the river. They were in the swamp. And at dawn the chase would begin once more.

Chapter 13   The Deadliest Killer

They worked through the swamp the following day, again heading east, facing into another day of bright sun and oppressive, moist heat.

This was greatly different from jungle travel, much less arduous, since the undergrowth was not nearly as dense and the hummocks of land, where the going was relatively easy, were close together. But they were constantly in and out of water, and all were soon wet from head to foot.

Tarzan had roused them in the gray dawn when thick mist swirled slowly through the swamp. "We must go on. Hawkins will have to take his chances on catching up with us."

He had been up a good part of the night, watching vainly for Hawkins. And Tarzan had been busy otherwise, also. He had completed the job that he had started yesterday morning just before Diana's capture, cutting up the black leopard skin and using it to make moccasins for the women.

They were wearing them today. Camage was limping a little but keeping uncomplainingly to the pace set by Tarzan.

Nor had she complained last night when she and Tarzan reached the camp, to discover that Fletcher had eaten all the meat kept in reserve against their possible appearance.

Tarzan apologized to her: "I'm sorry. I would try to find something for your supper, if I could. However, that's about the only edible animal in the swamp, and I cleaned out those here. Also, they're almost impossible to catch at night."

Penrod, absorbed in some weary thoughts of his own, apparently had not even noticed what Fletcher had done. But Diana was suddenly aware of his callous greed, and angrily cut short Fletcher's recital of what a hard time he had had floundering through the swamp. "Hal, you beast!" Then she came to the other woman. "Sit down, Camage. I'm going to fix your hair for you."

That act marked a change in Diana: a small one, true, but definitely for the better.

This morning, breakfast had been a tin of the processed beef, which was packed in gelatin and pretty tasteless, but Tarzan had forced them all to down several mouthfuls, then had allowed a sparing drink apiece from the flask in Penrod's bindle. The other flask, entrusted to Fletcher, was somewhere at the bottom of the river.

"Hear me now—and particularly you, Fletcher," Tarzan told them. "Don't drink a drop of swamp water! It could mean typhoid, at the very least."

They started out then, and had covered a considerable distance by sunup, all of them cold and wet and short-tempered. Then came the heat, and myriads of insects, with a rest halt while Tarzan found the pink cabbagelike plant and they applied its rubbery fluid to themselves.

On again, working from hummock to hummock, splashing through shallow pools, Tarzan at times back-tracked to work around some body of water that he thought too wide to cross. After a bit he checked the sun and began to veer toward the south.

There was beauty in the swamp for those who cared to look for it—masses of lilies and hyacinth, varying in color from pale white to deep crimson. Many orchidlike flowers flourished among the trees.

But there was deep quiet, also, and a sense of oppressive loneliness. The water was too shallow here to tempt crocodiles. Monkeys shunned swamps, and so there was no lively chatter from them. Some wildfowl were about, but on the wing, overhead. The only live things they came upon were various snakes that fled from them, with the exception of one coiled python that watched without much interest as they worked cautiously by.

Chetah, riding Tarzan's back, muttered in his ear that she liked this place even less by day than she had in the dark.

"I don't like it either," Tarzan told her. "But we should soon reach the veldt."

However, the morning hours passed and they were still in the swamp, its aspect unchanging, looking much the same as it had when they started.

A stop for a noon rest and a meager meal—more of the beef, plus several of the English biscuits apiece, another drink for all of them from the flask—and they pushed on.

There was no indication, all this while, of any pursuit. Tarzan had kept a sharp, constant watch, not only for the Oparians but also for Josiah Hawkins. Several times he called a halt while he climbed tall trees for a long look around them.

Penrod spoke to him, after one of those halts: "Do you think they caught Hawkins?"

"It looks that way," Tarzan answered. "He may have had some accident, though I doubt it. If he stayed free, I'm certain Hawkins would have found us sometime during the night. The only other possibility seems to be that he was captured."

There was an additional possibility Tarzan did not mention: that Hawkins had not been captured, but was nevertheless with the Oparians today—that he had joined them.

Considering all that had happened yesterday, that did not seem to make much sense. Hawkins had rescued Diana; he had worked as drivingly hard as Tarzan himself to escape down the river flowing from the lake.

Still, the day before in the jungle he had tried to slow down their flight, as though he wanted the Oparians to catch up with them. And he had been to Opar. He knew Ogonooroo, the great chief there.

It was something to keep in mind, the possibility that Hawkins was now working with the pursuing warriors.

Dick Penrod said, "It's tough to think of him in the hands of those people. Isn't there anything at all we can do about it?"

"Not now," Tarzan told him. "If he is a captive, Hawkins is in no immediate danger; take my word for that." He would be in no danger, if a captive, until arrival at Opar. "Once we reach the Ngamu River, I'll turn back if he hasn't reappeared, and search for him. But we have to get these women to safety first."

Penrod slowly nodded, jaw hardening. "You're right. Nothing must interfere with that."

They went on, still in the silent swamp. When the sun was two hours past noon, they suddenly came to a long strip of dry land stretching away before them, rather thickly timbered.

Diana exclaimed with relief. "How wonderful! We can get out of the water!"

She went ahead, splashing across a narrow pond, and up between two of the trees—then, a moment later, cried out, flailing with both hands. "Ugh! I've run into a spider web! And there are more here, a lot of them!"

Tarzan saw the webs, their gossamer skeins flashing in the sunlight. He called out sharply, "Mrs. Penrod, stand still!"

She twisted to look back at him. "Why—"

Camage Dean had followed her. She also looked around

as Tarzan hurried up to them. And Camage suddenly cried out, "There's one of them on me!"

She slapped at her neck. Tarzan caught her hand. "Stand absolutely still!" Then he reached out with care, forefinger against thumb; he snapped his finger and sent the spider that was crawling on her neck into the dirt.

Tarzan knelt to look at it. The spider began to scuttle away. Tarzan reached out with a twig to stop it. "Mrs. Penrod, did one of these get on you, too?"

"I—I don't think so," Diana said.

Penrod and Fletcher had joined them. Tarzan continued, "Don't come too close! But take a good look, all of you. This is the deadliest killer, for its size, in Africa. Black above—" he flipped the spider over on its back "—and red below. The natives call it Karwee, and fear it more than anything else. One bite from it, and, unless the poison is sucked out in a hurry, you will die very quickly. So watch for its web and stay well away from it. It is not a tarantula, but can jump for considerable distances just as a tarantula does."

Hal Fletcher muttered, "This is a fine time to tell us about it!"

"I know. I should have remembered that Karwee is

found only at the edge of swamps. Now that we know he is here, we can give him a wide berth."

Chetah had listened to their talk, which did not greatly interest her. Neither did spiders. What caught her attention was the fact that they had left the watery world of the swamp behind and had reached dry land again. Also, there were some trees here that she wanted to investigate. So she slid off Tarzan's back and headed in among them at a purposeful rolling gait, bindle bobbing about on her shoulder.

Tarzan said, "Come back here! Karwee can do you harm, also!"

Chetah glanced around in surprise. She chattered in protest, pointing upward to indicate where she meant to go.

Tarzan said, "No! Come back!"

Chetah resignedly obeyed. They retreated from the strip of dry land to the water again, working around the trees where those spider webs showed.

Tarzan stayed in the water. It was only a few inches deep. They splashed along. After a while, Penrod said, "Can't we leave this now?"

"Not yet," Tarzan answered.

"Why not?" Fletcher grumbled.

Tarzan said, "Look ahead, about thirty yards on your right, up on that low ridge."

They looked. Fletcher caught his breath, a gasping sound. Penrod's mouth tightened. What they saw was a lion, partially hidden in the long brownish grass: a big specimen, tawny in the bright sun, with a magnificent head, a full black mane.

He was watching them curiously, head cocked a little on one side.

Tarzan pointed to a circle of vultures wheeling slowly in the sky. "The scavengers are at work yonder, so Numa has eaten fairly recently and isn't likely to attack us. But he might, especially if we make any sudden move or loud sound. So keep walking at a steady pace and stay silent. Penrod, get ready to hurry the women out of the way if he should charge, while I go to meet him. . . ."

They plodded on. The women had seen the lion now, but the only sound from the group was Fletcher's ragged breathing.

They passed by a spot about ten yards in a straight line from where Numa stood, pretending unawareness of him. And he suddenly moved two steps closer.

Tarzan put hand to knife. He had fought Numa many

times in savage combat under circumstances such as this, his knife and maneuvering skill against the lion's teeth and fearsome claws. He would do so again if necessary, but he hoped Numa would not charge. Tarzan had the greatest possible respect for this great animal, and the deepest admiration as well.

Numa was the mighty, living symbol of all that made Africa the wonderful land that it was. He was brave, valorous, true to a code of his own, altogether something to be admired, from any standpoint.

The black-maned lion suddenly yawned, stretched himself out in the grass, and began to roll ecstatically, purring like a house cat on a hearth.

"Keep moving," Tarzan murmured. "He won't pay us any more attention if we just walk slowly away."

"Phew!" Dick Penrod whispered. "I'll admit I was plenty scared!"

"I wasn't," Fletcher growled. "And I just wish I had a gun, so I could put a bullet in him!"

"How big a gun?" Tarzan asked dryly. "One with enough bullets for the other six, also?"

Both men gaped at him. "S-Six?" Fletcher repeated, unbelievingly.

"Yes. A lioness, probably that one's mate, with three half-grown cubs, and two younger males."

They turned to look back at the high grass. "I don't see them," Fletcher muttered skeptically.

"I didn't see them, either," Tarzan said. "But they are there."

His nostrils had told him so. And now scent brought another warning. "I think it's fairly safe to go up that ridge," Tarzan told them. "And we have to turn aside; there are buffalo ahead of us."

They became visible, eight or ten of them, grazing along this trickle of water that led into the swamp, lifting their heads and shaking their horns as the scent of man reached them.

"They don't look much like American buffalo," Penrod remarked. "I've heard they're the most dangerous of African wild animals. Is that true, Tarzan?"

"All animals are dangerous if they are hurt and angry," Tarzan said. "A wounded buffalo will circle wide and stalk a man in the brush, charging him from behind. Also, they will fight for their young at any time—and there are young ones in that group yonder. Be sure to give them plenty of room."

He led them warily through the tall grass, up the ridge. As they reached the top of it, exclamations burst from all of them. As though a door had suddenly opened, the whole wonderful world of wild Africa was spread out before them.

It was the veldt, a great wide plain stretching far off to the south, with thick stretches of brush and trees at frequent intervals. And there were literally thousands of animals in sight, going about their daily business.

A great herd of impala went away from them, with long, graceful, curving leaps. A dozen giraffe moved together at their strange, stiltlike pace, heads gravely bobbing along eighteen or twenty feet above the ground. A hundred or more zebra swept past, running exuberantly—for no apparent reason, as zebras often do—with much braying and kicking up of heels. And there were other species, almost beyond counting, though Tarzan named some.

"Those are wildebeest yonder, the largest of the antelopes," he said. "Also bush gazelle, the small creatures with the spiked horns. Reedbuck and hartebeest and duiker and eland—about every kind of antelope is here, I think. More lions off in the distance; you can barely see them—they're dozing under those plane trees. Also about half a dozen elephants—"

"Where?" Diana demanded, shading her eyes. Then, "Yes, I see them!"

They were back among the trees also, swaying drowsily, squirting each other with dust, about a mile away.

"What a wonderful sight!" Camage breathed.

"They all seem to live together so peacefully," Diana said. "With those lions yonder, I wouldn't think there would be an antelope or zebra within miles."

"Those animals know where the lions are, and trust to their speed to escape, should one charge," Tarzan said. "This isn't, generally speaking, the hour when a lion is thinking about eating. The one we saw a while ago must have made his kill early this morning. The grazing creatures are obeying the law of the wild: eat or be eaten. And Nature gives them this opportunity to do their eating during the hours when the meat-hunters prefer to be lazy, in the shade."

Fletcher grumbled, "How much longer are we going to hang around here?"

"We'll move on now," Tarzan said. "Penrod, head eastward along this ridge."

Penrod nodded, but looked a little disappointed. "I was hoping we'd start across the veldt—make camp there

tonight and build a boma, just like I've read about in stories of Africa."

By boma, he meant an enclosing wall of thornbush. Tarzan smiled. "We'll camp on the veldt tonight, but without a boma."

Penrod looked surprised. "Why not?"

"For a very good reason. Numa is a most curious animal. When he sees a wall or fence, he must leap over it and find out what is on the other side. Once there, finding himself in an enclosed area, he becomes frightened and is liable to strike at anything that moves. So no boma. We will be much safer in the open."

Penrod grinned ruefully. "Well, that shatters a cherished illusion about Africa!"

They moved along the low ridge. And Tarzan was working on a mental problem.

Where were the Oparians? There had been no sign at all of them this day, no rattle of signal drums.

Had Waziru's force of warriors been so depleted during that hazardous trip down the river that he hadn't enough men left to follow them any farther? Had Waziru himself failed to survive the river trip, so that the band of Oparians was now without a leader?

There was some reason to hope one of these things might have happened, Tarzan thought. They continued along the ridge until it dipped down and merged with the veldt. Tarzan went ahead; they moved out onto the vast plain among the swarming herds of the wild. Some fled from them; some paid them no heed at all.

A mile passed, and another mile. Penrod spoke, a note of eagerness in his voice: "You think we're not being followed any longer, and can make it to the Ngamu now unmolested?"

"I'm hoping so," Tarzan answered. "About two days' journey, I think, from here—"

A sudden harsh barking interrupted him, then a frenzied yip from Chetah, who had wandered off ahead of the group. She came flying back, bindle dragging in the dirt, to leap at Tarzan, scramble up to his shoulders and huddle there, crying out in fear.

Baboons came bounding after her, the big dog-faced apes who were the mortal enemies of chimpanzees, banging knuckles in the dirt, barking their threats, coming quite close. Baboons feared only men with guns, and they could see there were none here.

Tarzan growled a throaty warning, and they all stopped,

to huddle and mutter in a conference, a dozen or more of them. Then a bearded patriarch announced a decision, and they began to come on again.

"Stand fast," Tarzan warned his party. "They want Chetah. I'll have to drive them away."

It might be a difficult task. Baboons, with their big teeth, were mean in a fight, and this many could cause trouble. Chetah tugged at Tarzan's hair, begging him to run, but he started toward them.

Then a curious thing happened. The old leader of the pack suddenly faced toward the south, head lifted, sniffing. The others did the same. They began to squeal uneasily.

"Tarzan, look yonder!" Dick Penrod cried.

Tarzan had already seen it—a great black cloud off to the south, with a flickering like heat lightning at its base. And he had scented the acrid tang of smoke that the baboons had also detected.

He studied that cloud for a moment as the baboons ran, all interest in Chetah forgotten. Then Tarzan spoke, his voice quiet and toneless:

"The veldt is burning, and the fire is coming in this direction. We must run from it, also—"

Chapter 14   Stampede

They fled back the way they had come, toward the north, and the creatures of the wild fled with them, running from the one enemy they feared more than any other—fire.

It was spreading with fearful speed, its roar now audible, like the thunder of a giant waterfall, brush and trees alike exploding into flame. And the smoke now swirled over them, thick and choking, with showers of scorching sparks. Diana cried out, beating at her hair; then Camage was doing the same.

Through the smoke darted a horde of animals, seeking to escape—the hoofed ones running in herds with a fearful bleating. With deep-throated roars, lions covered the ground in great leaps; Tarzan saw a lioness shepherding a brace of cubs, turning to snarl defiance at the flames.

Eight elephants rushed past, at the speed only elephants

could muster, trunks thrust straight out before them, trumpeting as they ran. Two hyenas scuttled along at the wobbling pace inflicted on them by their weak hindquarters. Tarzan noticed that one was caught and trampled by zebra that were galloping along like a black and white flood.

There was great danger from these fear-crazed animals. Gnus appeared out of the murk, hump-backed animals that looked like oxen; one brushed past Fletcher and knocked him flat. Tarzan jerked the man to his feet again, pulling him from the path of a herd of running hartebeest whose sharp hoofs would have cut him to pieces.

Monkeys and baboons and rock apes were included in the fleeing hordes, and many of them would not survive such a flight. Birds wheeled overhead, darting and dipping through the smoke; some, according to their strange impulses, flew back into the fire, there to perish.

"Stay together!" Tarzan shouted. Then, pointing, "Head that way!"

They could not return to the ridge, for the grass there would burn also. The animals would plunge on into the swamp, where many would bog down and die. Tarzan pushed his group toward the northeast, and the lifting ridges of barren land there.

As he ran he thought of the fire and its cause.

Tarzan had often seen fire on the veldt. Many of the grazing tribes burned it off every year, in the belief that it would mean better grass for their cattle. But this was not the season for such burning.

A conviction grew in him that the fire had been deliberately set. Two Oparians, moving fast, could have managed such an evil act.

And for a good reason—to cut off escape across the veldt for these whites they were pursuing. If this was true, it indicated the force of warriors had indeed been cut down. They must now accomplish by cunning what they could not do by force.

Tarzan ran on, with Chetah clinging to him, pushing the others. Penrod was helping Diana, and Tarzan lent a hand to Camage Dean. Fletcher was running by himself, well out in the lead.

A leopard streaked past, racing close to the ground, and yowled frenziedly as flying sparks singed it. Tarzan's skin was seared also. He ignored those bright spots of pain.

They struggled up a rise, through thick, chest-high grass.

"Keep going!" Tarzan called. This grass would burn, too. They went down the other side, splashed across a pool of stagnant water, a far outpost of the swamp, and in among moss-shrouded trees.

The smoke still swirled about them as they hurried through the trees, with Tarzan turning them now toward the east. The fire would not penetrate the swamp, but if the Oparians were here it was no place for them to linger.

Choking smoke and the many-voiced screaming from the hordes of fleeing animals—again scent and hearing failed Tarzan. When the attack came, it was Fletcher who saw them first and who turned and ran with a shrill cry of fear.

A bronze-skinned warrior bounded through the twilight gloom, racing after him. Tarzan shook off Chetah and moved quickly to intercept the Oparian. But Penrod was closer. He went at the man from the side. The Oparian whirled and jabbed him with a spear. Penrod leaped in close, swinging a fist. It connected solidly with the Oparian's jaw, and slammed him flat.

Another of them appeared, and another, running through the trees with ferocious shouts. One of them drove at Tarzan, thrusting with his spear, a low slash intended to hurt and down him. Tarzan evaded that thrust, then leaped in close as Penrod had, but not to use his fist. Instead, he hit with the edge of his hand at the Oparian's throat.

The carotid artery was there, and a solid blow against it could paralyze anyone for a space of several minutes. The Oparian dropped to the ground.

Penrod was now fighting two of them, still using his fists and showing both skill and courage. He downed one, but then was caught and himself downed from behind by the other, who lifted his spear to drive it into him.

Diana screamed. She was nearby, hands up to her cheeks, staring fearfully. Tarzan reached the spearman and seized him, with a twist and a hard shove that sent him reeling away. He went headfirst into a nearby shallow pool.

Penrod scrambled up. Two more of them were coming to the attack. Penrod hit one in a low tackle that slammed him hard against a tree trunk. An arrow flashed past Tarzan. He caught the Oparian who had fired it, and threw him into the pool, snatching away his bow and breaking it as he did so.

The fellow Penrod had first hit was lurching away into the swamp, holding his jaw with both hands. The one Tarzan had seized with that hard twist followed him, arm hanging limply. The bowman followed him.

The second one Penrod had downed ran, also. And the

warrior Penrod had tackled wriggled free, saw Tarzan coming at him, and took to his heels.

It had all happened in only a few seconds. Penrod regained his feet, holding his left arm. "Got nicked by that first one," he said. "But I think I broke his jaw!"

Tarzan thought so, too. And he had himself dislocated the shoulder of the one who had gone away with arm dangling. Those two would do no more fighting for some time.

Six of them, he told himself. Could they be all that were left of the more than twenty who had left Opar? Or were there others, scattered along the edge of the swamp, dispersed because they could not be sure where the whites, retreating from the veldt fire, would reappear?

Diana was staring at her husband as though she had never seen him before. "Dick, you were wonderful!" she exclaimed.

Then, as Camage removed her jacket, peppered with holes from flying sparks, and began to tear it apart to bandage Penrod's arm, Diana spoke again. "Let me take care of him, Camage . . . please."

Fletcher was coming back, looking down at the ground and wearing a hangdog expression—with no bluster this time. He had shown his cowardice, running away during that moment of terrible danger. All of them knew it.

Chetah called excitedly for Tarzan's attention; she was running off under the trees, following the Oparian Tarzan had dropped with the throat-blow. The savage was now groggily trying to crawl away on his hands and knees.

Tarzan went after him. He had questions this Oparian was going to answer: how many of his kind were left in the swamp, and whether Hawkins was with them.

The warrior struggled up and started to run. Half a dozen paces behind, Tarzan heard him suddenly scream and saw his body become rigid, saw him pitch to the ground and writhe there, under spider webs spun thickly between the trees.

Tarzan knelt beside him. He saw the spider against the bronze back close to the neck—reached out to flick it away, then used his knife hurriedly to cut a crisscross in the flesh at the tiny puncture wound. He bent to suck the Oparian's blood, to spit it out and suck again.

And to no avail. The spider's poison had been injected too close to the heart. The man soon lay still, unstirring. Tarzan felt for a pulse and found none.

The others had followed him, stopping and watching silently at a little distance. Tarzan turned to them. "Don't come any closer. This is Karwee's work. The venom took effect very swiftly. . . . Penrod, are you all right?"

"Sure!" Dick Penrod was pale but steady. Diana, standing beside him, was still working on the bandage she had put over his cut arm. He added, "I'm ready to back you up if they tackle us again."

"We'll hope that won't happen," Tarzan said. "Lead out toward the east."

Penrod studied him. "We're going toward the mountains?"

"Yes. That veldt fire will spread far before it burns out, and we're blocked off from the south. We'll have to reach the Ngamu through the mountains," Tarzan said.

They would be going toward Opar, which was somewhere in those mountains. But it had to be done. No other way was open to them.

At gray dawn, three mornings later, Tarzan sat on a ledge outside of a shallow cave that was part way up a bleak ridge, fingers flying as he braided another rope.

The mountains rose up precipitately above him to the east, black and forbidding at this hour, but with some higher peaks brushed rose and pink by the distant rising sun.

Chetah yawned nearby, struggling to stay awake. She knew that the making of the rope, on which Tarzan had worked all night, indicated he was planning a new venture, and Chetah had stayed up with him; she meant to go along when he left this place.

A stir sounded from within the cave, and Penrod came out. His clothes were rags and tatters. He was gaunt, with smudges of weariness under his eyes. But adversity had put into him strength and sureness he had not possessed that day the plane had crashed. Tarzan now approved of Dick Penrod. He had become a man who could be relied on in any emergency.

Penrod eyed the rope and lifted his brows questioningly. Tarzan did not pause in his braiding. He was using strands of a hemplike plant that grew thickly alongside streams in this upland country. "Get the others out here, Penrod. I've something to say to all of you."

They appeared, one at a time. Camage and Diana now wore skirts fashioned from the bolt of red cloth Tarzan had salvaged from the plane; he had used a thorn as a needle and other plant fibers as thread, putting the skirts together. Diana also had on her short coat, and Camage was wearing Dick Penrod's suede jacket.

They were both worn down by the rigors of the hard journey, but they had managed to bear up surprisingly well—had kept themselves clean and neat. The contents of Camage's bag had spared them from too much blistering by the African sun.

Dick Penrod had also kept himself clean, bathing and washing his tattered clothes whenever opportunity offered. Fletcher, who came out of the cave last, had not. He had turned slovenly and indifferent. Since that moment when he had run away from the fight in the swamp there had been a change in Fletcher, and it was obviously not for the better.

He scratched himself now, giving Tarzan a surly look. "I still say if we'd gone back to hunt for Hawkins in the swamp, he'd have gotten us to that river by this time. Now I suppose you're going to ask us to climb those mountains —and I won't do it. I've got to rest!"

"You'll get some rest today, Fletcher," Tarzan interrupted. Then he ignored him, speaking to the others: "I think the Ngamu must be nearby, possibly no more than about two days' journey distant, east and south beyond those mountains. But you're all too worn down for the climbing that will be necessary to find it. So I'm going on alone. I'll locate the Ngamu and the easiest way to reach it. Then I'll come back here."

He stood up and began to coil his rope—about a hundred feet of it, as before, as much as could be readily handled. Tarzan continued, "I picked this cave because it's well hidden. Stay here. You've plenty of food and water for several days—" he had brought in an ibex, a mountain gazelle, last night, and they still had some of their tinned rations. "And if anybody should happen along—*anybody*—" he emphasized the word strongly "—don't reveal yourselves to them!"

The two women and Penrod nodded their understanding. Fletcher grunted indifferently. Diana, standing beside her husband, gave Fletcher an angry look.

Tarzan looped the coil of rope over his left shoulder. "That's about all. I'll try to return before dark today—but by sometime tomorrow, sure."

"Good luck!" Camage said. The Penrods offered the same wish. Fletcher scowled and said nothing.

Tarzan started to turn away then, but paused for a glance at Chetah, smiling. She was dozing, chin on chest, bindle over her shoulder; the little chimpanzee had not let go of it for a moment.

"Let her sleep," Tarzan said. "I couldn't have taken Chetah along, anyway, where I'm going."

He climbed steadily at a fast pace, up the steeply lifting face of one of the great mountains.

Tarzan paused occasionally to look back and down. There was some mist below him for a while, until the sun cleared the peaks and burned it away. He could see most of the barren upland country they had crossed during those two days and a half of arduous travel after they had left the swamp for the second time.

Perhaps they had shaken off the Oparians for good, during that hard trek. There had been no sign of pursuit, no drum talk by night when the glow of the still-burning veldt had been ruddy against the sky.

There had been very little cover available in the rising country they were crossing. Tarzan had constantly hoped there would be a chance to turn southward across the veldt. But the far spread of the fire had ruled that out. To reach the Ngamu, and the river boats plying that stream, they had to go through the mountains.

They had encountered moments of danger from snakes and leopards, as well as other animals that had been driven northward by the fire—buffalo, singed and bad-tempered, a herd of elephants that had driven them to shelter for several hours in the deep dry bed of a creek, and a rhino that had charged them.

Tarzan had worked the rhino away from the others. It had worn itself out vainly trying to run him down, and had at last gone off to find its way, he hoped, to some place where it could survive.

Tarzan crossed a towering high ridge where the air was thin and cold. More peaks, higher still and topped by snow-caps, towered above him. A distant ibex whistled shrilly and ran away from him, bounding up a sheer cliff where there seemed to be no path at all.

A few miles north he saw what appeared to be a pass cutting into and perhaps through this massive range. Tarzan marked its position and turned eastward, climbing again. Soon he found a wall of rock squarely before him.

It was several hundred feet high. Tarzan studied the wall with care for some minutes, then began to scale the mass of rock. At least half a day, he thought, would be required to go around it.

There were seams here and there, split open by frost, and he worked his way upward along them, clinging by fingers and toes, occasionally hanging on only by finger-tip pressure as he swung himself ever higher. Presently he reached a point where no more seams were available to him.

With an almost sheer fall of two hundred or more feet below, Tarzan clung to the wall and looked up. He saw a rock spur fifty feet above him and off to his right.

Tarzan used the rope now, shifting it from one hand to another as he shook out a loop. He made a right-hand cast toward the spur. It fell short. He tried again, feeding out more rope, and missed again, patiently brought the loop back and tried once more.

On his fifth cast the loop fell over the spur. Tarzan pulled hard then, testing until he was sure the rope would hold and the spur would not break. Next he gripped the rope with both hands, swung to the right on it like a pendulum until he was under the spur, then walked up the rock wall to it.

The spur was wide enough to stand on. Tarzan now studied the wall above him again. Another fifty feet up there seemed to be a ledge jutting out from the face of the rock. Tarzan began to throw his loop upward again, with the same careful patience, until he put it over some projection where it held.

Now he could not walk up the rock wall, which slanted outward above him. Tarzan had to climb the rope itself, hand over hand with it wrapped around one leg in case his hands should slip, hanging in space with that steep drop below him.

He was halfway up when, with a screech and a shrill whistling sound from fiercely beating wings, a great male mountain eagle suddenly plummeted out of the blue to attack him.

At the sound of its screech Tarzan instantly twisted toward the bird, gauged its direction and speed in a split second, and pendulumed out of its path. Slashing talons and the snap of its curved beak missed him by inches. The sweep of a wing beat against his left arm with the force of a club.

It banked away, gained altitude, and poised for another assault, silvered wing tips and crest glinting in the sunlight. Tarzan climbed hurriedly, but he could not reach the ledge before it attacked again, plummeting down as before, a dive with wings folded until the last moment, when they shot out to serve as a brake while its talons slashed at his face.

This time Tarzan gauged that dive. His right fist lashed

at the bird, a move even faster than the rake of its claws, a jarring blow against its breast that sent the eagle tumbling in a whirling fall on downward.

It recovered a scant few feet from the ground at the base of the wall, and began the sweep of wings to gain height again.

Tarzan climbed on up to the ledge quickly, and saw the reason for the attack—a female on a nest of sticks. The bird shrieked at him but did not leave her eggs.

The ledge extended for some distance. Tarzan pulled up and coiled his rope, moving northward along it. The male made one more dive at him. Tarzan flipped the noose at the great bird, which veered away in fright, then banked and wheeled above him, apparently content now only to watch, since he had not harmed its mate.

Tarzan found a slope that he could climb, and reached the top of the rock wall.

This was a very high point in the mountain mass. It had taken him half a day to come this far. He looked south and eastward first—and, far in the distance, at least a hundred miles away, he saw a line of green at the edge of the horizon beyond the mountains that he knew must be the Ngamu River.

Then Tarzan faced about, to search for the pass he had noticed before. It was visible northward, winding between the great peaks. Tracing it eastward by sight, he suddenly saw something else.

A deep, very deep canyon first, spanned by a rope bridge —and, beyond the canyon, dwellings that clung to the side of a towering cliff where two giant figures were carved out of solid rock.

About twenty miles from where he stood, in a straight line, Tarzan estimated, probably much closer than that by the pass below. And he had never felt more certain of anything than of his instant guess as to what it was—the legendary, hidden city of Opar.

Chapter 15   Ogonooroo's Trap

The trip back to the cave where he had left the others took nearly as much time as the climb upward, though Tarzan hurried his return, finding a way down the rock wall that avoided the eagles.

It was about two hours short of sunset when he again approached the cave.

The pass through the mountains could not be used, though Tarzan had traced a path, following it, that would surely lead to the Ngamu. The pass ran too near Opar. They had to work around the mountains and across the burned veldt—a much harder journey, twice as far as through the pass, across country where all game had been driven away by the fire.

They would be forced to eat their scanty rations and then go hungry. But it was a journey that had to be undertaken at once. As worn as the others were, they had to find the strength, somehow, to survive. It was a grim prospect.

Approaching the cave, Tarzan called, "Penrod!"

There was no answer. He hurried on, noticing with sudden coldness signs that others had also approached it today. There were marks of bare footprints in the dirt, eight or more natives; it was hard to estimate for sure at a quick glance. And among them were the prints of a man who had worn shoes.

The cave was empty. But in and around it were indications of a fierce struggle, probably put up by Penrod. He had been overwhelmed. And now they were gone, all of them, taken away toward the north by those intruders.

A shrill, relieved call sounded; Chetah came bounding down the ridge. She waved an arm and chattered excitedly as she approached, trying to tell what had happened here. Men had come. Somehow they had discovered the cave. Chetah had prudently retreated, to wait for Tarzan's return.

She made a disconsolate face and put an arm over her eyes—her way of expressing fear for the fate of the four who had been seized. And she tried to tell him something else.

"I think I know what you mean. There was a white man

with them," Tarzan said. Then, "Come on! Up! We must follow their trail."

Chetah leaped to his back, and he set out at a fast lope, a pace he could maintain for hours. Chetah hung on with some difficulty. She still clung to her bindle.

The tracks were easy to follow for a while. The four whites had been pushed along fast by their captors. Studying the footprints, pausing to examine a place where grass had been crushed flat, Tarzan estimated that the capture had taken place sometime after noon. They could not be very far ahead of him.

Then the trail led into a rocky defile and vanished. But there was something in plain sight to guide Tarzan on— Hal Fletcher's hat.

He gave that a thoughtful look, plunged into the defile, and emerged from it a mile northward. Here a number of shallow canyons began, spreading out like the opened fingers of a hand. Which one had they gone into? Again there was a sign to guide him: a piece of red cloth torn from one of the women's skirts, lying in plain sight once more.

Tarzan frowned now, but went into that canyon, continuing on. It ran quite a distance, until its walls flattened out and he found himself on a high, rocky plain where no footprints showed anywhere. The mountains rose sheer on his right.

Another sign showed the direction they had taken: Penrod's cigarette lighter, glittering in the late afternoon sunlight. Tarzan bent to scoop it up, tucked it under his leopard skin.

Three or four miles farther, slanting across the plain, with more items to mark the way they had gone—small pieces of cloth, a lipstick from Camage Dean's bag, a tin of biscuits—and Tarzan reached the beginning of the pass.

It slanted steeply upward, a narrow opening that led through the mountains.

At early twilight a cold wind began to blow. Chetah muttered protestingly, squirming about.

"I know. And it's going to get colder," Tarzan said. "Just hold on and keep quiet."

He settled to a steady, shuffling trot as the air grew thinner, increasing the demands on his lungs, with wariness for an ambush at every spot where one might have been set for him.

Those conveniently placed signs had not deceived Tarzan for a moment. They had been deliberately spotted to draw him on. He could guess whose idea that had been—

Josiah Hawkins'—and also that it must have been Fletcher who had offered the information that Tarzan would return to the cave.

He pressed on, with the mountains soaring up, gray and black in these moments just before dusk. Tarzan had not slept for many hours, had not eaten since dawn today, but he gave no thought to these things as he followed the constantly rising pass.

At last, with stars now beginning to appear in the sky, he encountered one more sign: Diana's coat, placed on a boulder and weighted down with a rock.

Tarzan's lips tightened. They could have used something else; she had need of the coat. And what did it mean?

He searched about, and found a hidden trail nearby that slanted away from the pass, working up a steep ridge. Tarzan climbed that. There was still enough light for him to note that the trail was old but little used. The Oparians, he thought, must have kept to their mountains; there had been no need for them to leave those high fastnesses until the time came to go down to the plains and jungle and search for whites to sacrifice in their religious ceremonies.

Tarzan reached the top of the ridge and saw Opar, two miles away, with those figures carved from the rock cliff gigantic in this moment of late twilight. They were prob-ably many centuries old—seated figures resembling the statues of ancient Egyptian gods that Tarzan had once seen at Luxor on the Nile, far north of here.

A stairway of some sort seemed to rise between them. Tarzan noted this, and then turned his attention to a quick survey of the rest of Opar.

The place, he saw, occupied a shelf against the flank of one of the great mountains, whose peak, only a few hundred feet above the towering cliff, had the ragged aspect of a dead volcano.

Immediately before it was the deep canyon, probably wrenched open by some mighty convulsion of the earth in ages past, perhaps the same one that had caused the Great Rift of Kenya. The bridge that crossed it at the north end of Opar consisted of rope cables swinging between massive timbers, supporting a footpath. It seemed about a hundred feet long, and appeared to be the only means of reaching the ancient city.

Beyond the bridge Tarzan made out a wide trail that followed the canyon northward, probably a route used for trade with other mountain tribes.

The dwellings he had noticed before were built against

the face of the cliff. They were piled one on top of the other, in places as many as five high, like apartment houses; a necessity, since there was no room to build anywhere else. They seemed to be constructed of wood, and appeared to be very old. Long ladders allowed entrance to the upper huts.

These things Tarzan encompassed in a rapid glance, and then frowned as he studied what was going on beyond the canyon.

People were milling around over there with a good deal of loud shouting. They carried torches which made many bright spots of light in the deepening gloom, and they seemed to be moving toward the south end of the narrow shelf on which Opar was built, heading toward a great fire which suddenly flamed up.

Someone began to beat on a drum. Not signal talk, but deep, reverberating booms, measured, many seconds elapsing between beats. A loud chanting began. It had a boastful, exultant sound.

Chetah, who had been silent for some time, shivering from the cold, suddenly stirred and muttered fretfully. She did not like what she saw and heard. Chetah did not want to go any farther.

"I don't like it either," Tarzan said. "But we must go on."

He cautiously began to descend the ridge then, but not following the trail that led downward. Instead, Tarzan worked through rocks and a thick, scrubby sort of brush that was apparently the only thing growing at this high altitude.

The bridge must have been reached and crossed by the Oparian warriors and their captives, Tarzan told himself. But the signs so plentifully left for him to find must mean a trap was waiting for him, either between the ridge and that deep gorge yonder, or on its far side.

Tarzan did not think the Oparians would care to risk letting him cross the bridge and reach their city. The trap must be somewhere on this side of the canyon. But how, in the dark night now closing down, was he to locate it, render it harmless, and go on?

He stopped, with a murmur to Chetah, who reluctantly scrambled down from his back. Tarzan knelt among inky shadows cast by some boulders, and spent several moments in a careful scrutiny of the slope below.

But even his sharp eyes detected nothing, no stir of movement anywhere.

In Opar the booming of that drum kept up. The parade

of torches continued, a flowing river of light, and the chanting grew louder.

There was a strong feeling in Tarzan of time growing very short. That procession must be wending its way to the place of sacrifice.

He found his thoughts suddenly going back to the strange signal he had heard at the time of Diana's rescue, and again the night in the swamp. That signal had some significance that might aid him now. At least, nothing was to be lost by making it.

Tarzan reached out to touch his hand to Chetah's mouth. "Keep very quiet," he murmured. "Make no sound at all."

Then he felt about him, picked up a fist-sized rock, and tapped it against a boulder in the sequence that he had memorized: two short, one long, a short and a long.

The clicking sounds, sharp and staccato, rang far through the night. And there was an instant response from below Tarzan, a stir of movement and a surprised grunt, with somebody rising there, probably leaving a hiding place picked with care.

Then a voice from elsewhere, farther away: "Omoru, take care! We were ordered to stay hidden and wait!"

"Im shigra! We were told that, yes—to wait for *m-tu*

zanje, a white man who would come along." It was a growling answer. "But there is another order—to answer that
signal of Ogonooroo, whenever and wherever we hear it
made. I go to do that."

The man who had spoken came up toward Tarzan, moving at a cautious pace, someone who cast a big shadow.

Tarzan waited for him. The signal of Ogonooroo which
had to be answered; this was interesting information.

The man prowled close to him and stopped. He spoke
again: "Who made the call of five, sacred to the great chief?
Speak quickly, and if it is not your right to use that signal,
your head will roll in the pit of skulls!"

Tarzan eased the coil of rope from his shoulder. He hit
the man from the side, a noiseless rush and leap in the now
thick darkness. An arm whipped about the Oparian's
throat, tightening under his chin, instantly silencing him.

The man reacted galvanically, bucking and twisting, trying to shake Tarzan off. He was big and powerful, which
was probably the reason he had been chosen for this assign-
ment, and he used all his strength in an effort to break free.

But the pressure of Tarzan's throttling arm increased,
cutting off all air from the Oparian's lungs. It was a con-
test of strength and will that ended when the man suddenly

sagged limply, all resistance ended. Tarzan held on for seconds longer, until certain it was no trick and the man was really senseless. Then he lowered him to the ground, returned to where he had left the rope, cut short lengths from one end, and tied the Oparian up, with a loop about his head and thrust into his open mouth to keep him silent.

Again Tarzan went to the boulders. He made the signal of Ogonooroo, adding the combination of taps that everywhere in drum talk meant, "Come quickly. I am in trouble."

It brought two more of them out of hiding, muttering to each other worriedly as they slowly started up the slope. One of them raised his voice in a call to the fellow who was now on his face in the dust, ankles and wrists tightly bound: "Omoru! What have you found? Speak!"

Tarzan chirped almost inaudibly to Chetah, an order for her to stay put. He slid out of the boulders and went to meet them, closely hugging the ground, as quiet as a drifting shadow.

They were silhouetted by the flare of torches from Opar. One held a spear, the other a bow with an arrow notched and ready. Tarzan charged again.

This time he did not achieve complete surprise. The spearman slashed at him, and the iron point of his weapon grazed

Tarzan's side. But the arrow of the other never left its bow. Tarzan reached out with both hands, gripping their necks, and drove them forcibly against each other. There was a chunking sound, their heads colliding, and the warriors spilled down, knocked out, as limp and senseless as the other warrior up the ridge.

Tarzan knelt beside them with a low, tense command: "Chetah, bring the rope! Hurry!"

She obeyed, scampering to join him, dragging the coil of rope. Tarzan bound these two, also—wrists tied behind their backs, then their ankles, plus a loop of rope pulling their limbs tightly together—with knots they could pick at all night and not untie. Then he gagged them.

These two were big men, also, undoubtedly picked for size and fighting ability. Tarzan made Ogonooroo's call one more time. There was no reply. These three represented the force that had been posted in hiding to watch for and overwhelm him.

Chetah muttered an inquiring sound. She was excited now, eager for the next move.

"We are going across that bridge," Tarzan said.

And it might not be easy, he told himself. There were probably guards watching it.

Chapter 16   Opar

But there were no guards at this end of the bridge. They were posted at the other end; Tarzan could see them, two warriors with flaming torches. It was an arrangement probably logical enough from the Oparian point of view, since anyone trying to cross on the narrow footpath suspended between swaying ropes would be immediately visible and the alarm would be sounded at once.

What the Oparians had never taken into account was that the bridge could be crossed without walking on that footpath. It was the means that Tarzan chose. He went over the canyon edge underneath the bridge, reached up, gripped the outer edges of the rough planks that had been laid to make the footpath, and started to swing himself across, hanging by his hands.

Chetah could not understand this strange performance,

but she came after him, somewhat hampered by her bindle.

Tarzan muttered, "Why don't you get rid of that thing?"

She protested at such a suggestion. Chetah meant to hold onto the bindle and the brass ring in it, until she could display them to the forest chimps along the Ruwenzori, even if it meant now that she had to crab along after Tarzan, using one hand and one foot. At that, her agility was not much decreased.

"Oh, all right; you can keep the bindle," Tarzan said to keep her quiet, and they moved on together.

He had a sense of great depth below his dangling feet, and glanced down, but it was too dark for him to estimate how deep this chasm was. It must drop far beneath him, however, a natural barrier that had made Opar immune to attack.

Tarzan worked on with a steady shifting of his hands. His weight was making the bridge sway and tilt a little, but there was some wind also shaking the structure, and the swaying passed unnoticed.

Chetah was muttering again, wanting to know why they were working so hard at this when they could climb up and walk across. She grew a bit careless. A hand slipped; she pitched sideways and hung head down, held only by the tight grip of one small foot.

Tarzan let go with his right hand and reached out quickly, gripping rough coarse hair and the loose skin underneath it. Chetah squealed protestingly, squirming and reaching up to catch hold again. She scolded him then, somewhat miffed that Tarzan should have thought she might fall.

"Keep quiet," Tarzan breathed. "And don't be careless again!"

They worked on and reached the far side of the canyon without further incident. Tarzan felt firm ground under his feet. Chetah dropped down beside him.

The torches held by the two guards made a ruddy pool of light only a few feet away. Those guards were talking together:

"—of all nights in the year, this is the one we had to be chosen to stand guard here!" one of the Oparians was grumbling.

"Well, with that fire burning so brightly, we can see the sacrifices," the second one answered. "And we will take part in the great feast afterward!"

"What was done with the four whites?" the first guard asked gruffly.

"They were taken to the secret place," the second one said. "Ogonooroo is there. They will all come out again when the moon appears."

The rising moon was dimly visible behind a bank of clouds. Tarzan began silently to swing wide around the two guards.

As he did so, one of them shifted position, looking across the bridge. "Omoru and those with him who wait for the last of the whites are very quiet. Perhaps we should hail them."

The other guard snorted. "They are quiet so the white will fall into their trap. Omoru will catch that *m-tu zanje;* he is the strongest and most cunning warrior in Opar, after Waziru. He will squeeze the white man until his ribs crack like dead sticks!"

Tarzan left them behind, moving quickly away through darkness. The dwellings of Opar seemed deserted. All of its people, he thought, must be clustered around a mound that he now saw, a half mile or so to southward, where the great fire burned, the torches flared, the booming of the drum continued, and the chanting went on.

At the top of the mound were some strange-looking objects silhouetted by the fire. They were made either of

wood or stone and in the shape of the letter T. There were
five of them in a row, and it was not hard to guess their
purpose. They were waiting for the victims who were to
be sacrificed to the blood moon.

It was difficult to estimate the number of people gathered
about that mound—several hundred, perhaps. The people
of Opar, slaves of their savage pagan religion, eagerly
awaiting the spilling of blood to their gods.

One of those guards had spoken of a secret place. Tarzan studied the two giant seated figures carved from solid
rock, and the stairway that rose between them, thinking
of the probability that those stone steps led to some sort of
temple. He went up them, with Chetah scrambling along
behind.

The two statues stared sightlessly at the dark mountains.
They were definitely Egyptian, probably thousands of
years old. And the Oparians, Tarzan thought, were probably of Egyptian stock, perhaps isolated in these mountains long ago, surviving on this narrow shelf below the
high cliff and protected by the deep abyss over which they
had swung the rope bridge.

Tarzan reached the top of the stone steps and discovered
they led nowhere, ending against the face of the cliff. It

was a bitter disappointment, with time running out fast. He turned and started down again, was about halfway to the bottom when he heard an echo of voices coming from somewhere.

Tarzan hurriedly investigated. He discovered an opening in the solid rock near the steps, a narrow, vertical slit; the voices came from there. By turning sideways he could squeeze into it, a passage of some sort. Tarzan worked his way along the slit—ten feet, a dozen, even farther. Chetah, following him, muttered complainingly; she did not like dark, enclosed places. But she was too curious about all this to wait for Tarzan outside.

He became aware of light ahead. The voices were growing louder.

And Tarzan stopped, where the passage through the rock ended. He saw them, before and somewhat below him—an eerie scene, lighted by a number of torches. He realized now that this slit through solid rock had been gouged out as an air vent, and that he was looking into a vast cavern which was the core of an ancient volcano, the secret place mentioned by the guard at the bridge.

Dick and Diana Penrod were there, Hal Fletcher and Camage Dean, held by Oparian warriors. Waziru was

present—also Josiah Hawkins, rifle half-raised and finger
warily on the trigger.

This much Tarzan noticed at first glance. They had all
entered this place through some entrance at ground level.
And then he saw the ivory.

It was dimly visible in the background, row on row of
tusks, piled up like cordwood, some of them of unbelievable size, as Hawkins had said. Hundreds and thousands of
those tusks, the accumulation of centuries, and of incalcu-
lable value. Any one of them would bring thousands of
either English pounds or American dollars, at Djibouti, for
shipment to India.

There was another man in the cave, squatty of size,
grossly fat, loaded down with ivory ornaments. He, like
Waziru, wore a headdress of green and scarlet feathers. It
did not require Hawkins' deferential manner or the use
of his name to identify him to Tarzan. He was the great
chief of Opar, Ogonooroo.

Hawkins was talking fast and persuasively to Ogonooroo.
He was reciting the story of Josiah Hawkins, liar and
traitor.

Hawkins had indeed been to Opar previously, hunting
through the mountains for the great ivory treasure. He had

dickered with Ogonooroo, who had promised him one ivory tusk of his own choosing for each white he delivered to Opar.

"That was your promise, Ogonooroo!" Hawkins said. "I call on you now to fulfill it!"

Hawkins had gone to Nairobi, where he had persuaded Diana Penrod, through Fletcher, to fly to Opar. There was a place in the mountains nearby where a plane might be landed. It was Hawkins' plan to betray the four whites to Ogonooroo and collect his reward.

But his plan had misfired. The plane had crashed. Tarzan had appeared. Hawkins had learned from the drum talk that a party of Oparians was near, and had tried to deliver the others, including Tarzan, into their hands. He had signaled to them by the fire that morning at the canyon, and had tried to hold the whites back as they fled through the jungle. He had shot the Oparian warrior as another signal, also wanting to shut the man up before Tarzan shook damaging information from him as to the location of Opar.

But there was one thing Hawkins had not known, and that was the presence of Waziru as leader of the Oparians.

Waziru had objected to Ogonooroo's act in letting Hawkins leave Opar after his previous visit, counseling that instead Hawkins should be kept prisoner, to be used as a sacrificial victim at the time of the blood moon. Hawkins knew that, and there had been bitter enmity between the two men. But there obviously was none now.

What had happened to bring those two together? Tarzan listened intently as Hawkins continued talking.

At the crocodile river, Hawkins had used Ogonooroo's call, learned by him when he was in Opar before, to talk to Diana's captors. From them he had discovered that Waziru, who was skeptical about Hawkins ever returning to Opar, was seeking whites in the same area where five had been captured last year.

Hawkins had then demanded the release of Diana. He knew that he must move fast to elude Waziru and reach Opar ahead of him, or he would himself become a captive for sacrifice to the blood gods. The Oparian warriors holding Diana had not dared deny anything to one who made Ogonooroo's call; they had let Hawkins have her.

This explained Hawkins' eagerness to escape down the wild canyon river; he had been running from Waziru. But in the swamp he had turned back to check on the Oparians, again making Ogonooroo's call. He had learned that Waziru had lost ten men in the river, and those left were not in very good shape—which might explain why they had not put up more of a fight against Tarzan and Penrod the following day.

The weakness of Waziru's position had changed everything. Hawkins, who by then feared that he alone could not overcome Tarzan's strength and intelligence, had decided on a bold move.

"I proposed to Waziru that we work together, great chief," he said to Ogonooroo. "And he agreed."

Waziru nodded. With so few men left, he had needed Hawkins' help and cunning. But, Tarzan thought, there must have been some other reason why Waziru had agreed. What was that reason?

It had been Hawkins' scheme to burn the veldt, so Tarzan and those with him could not cross it. Waziru had ordered the attempt to capture them in the swamp, which had failed.

"That was the wrong thing to do," Hawkins said. "I had told Waziru that they must head for the mountains, since it was the only way they could go, that we must follow and capture them near Opar."

"They moved very fast. They almost escaped us," Waziru muttered. "And they hid themselves very well."

"I also told you," Hawkins said with a smirk, "that there was one among them who would betray where they were hiding, when we knew they were somewhere near, if I went ahead and called his name. Did it not work out that way?"

Camage, Fletcher, and the Penrods were standing in attitudes of near-exhaustion; being hustled along to Opar over that pass had left them badly worn. Dick Penrod, listening to the talk, not understanding but apparently realizing what it meant, spoke with sudden thick-voiced anger: "Blast you, Fletcher, for not staying in the cave and keeping quiet, as Tarzan told us to do! You're the one who had to rush out and yell when you heard Hawkins calling!"

So it was Fletcher who had betrayed them.

Ogonooroo spoke for the first time. He had a thin, reedy voice. "You say there is another white who will be along, so that the full number of five will be sacrificed tonight?"

"That's right!" Hawkins assured him. "I left a plain trail for him. He must have headed for Opar as fast as he could follow, soon as he got back and found that cave empty!"

"I ordered Omoru and two others to wait for him beyond

the bridge," Waziru said. "They know their heads will roll in the pit of skulls if they do not seize him."

"If the gods so will, it shall be done," Ogonooroo said. "Now, quiet, all, while I speak to them."

He turned to the ivory hoard and lifted both arms high, head tilted as though listening. Presently his voice rose again:

"Hear me! For many times the lives of many men, Opar was great! The caravans passing through the mountains from the flat country were raided and their ivory seized, to be brought to this secret place. But now no caravans come. The gods have told me they are angry— that we had grown soft, forgetting our past. They said we must become hard again, use the seven days of torture to choose our fiercest warriors, and send them to capture whites for sacrifice at the time of the blood moon—white, since that is the color of ivory, and to the number of five, which is the sacred number of the gods. Do these things, they said, and ivory will come to us once more. Opar will be great again!"

Tarzan grunted. So this was the reason for the sacrifices. And neither they nor anything else could bring the caravans through the mountains again, for the vast elephant herds that had supported the ivory trade were gone forever. No more tusks would be added to the hoard in this cave.

Ogonooroo faced around again. "We go now to the place of sacrifice," he announced.

"What about my ivory?" Hawkins demanded. "One tusk for each white delivered here, and men to carry them out of the mountains!"

"You will have your answer when the moon is high," Ogonooroo said. "Waziru, bring Hawkins with you." Then he waddled away. The guards started shoving the others after him. But Dick Penrod resisted.

"Hawkins," Penrod said, voice hoarse and pleading, "I don't care about myself, but if there's any humanity in you, make these devils let the women go free!"

Hawkins laughed at him jeeringly. Penrod wrenched himself from his guards' clutches, leaped at Hawkins, and swung a fist at his face.

It brought blood to Hawkins' mouth. He hit Penrod with the stock of his rifle, driving him down to his knees. The guards dragged Penrod away.

Hawkins and Waziru were left alone in the cavern, Waziru holding a torch. Hawkins muttered, "I don't like the way things are going—have got a feeling that if Tarzan isn't caught by the time of sacrifice, Ogonooroo is liable to have me grabbed and put on the rack with those others!"

"*Im shigra!* That may be. The gods demand five victims," Waziru said.

"Which is something that nobody got around to telling me when I was here before!" Hawkins growled.

"The gods told Ogonooroo then only that you should bring whites to Opar—not that he should reveal the secret number to you," Waziru said.

"Well, if I had known, I'd sure have brought one more from Nairobi!" Hawkins said.

Then he added slyly, "Waziru, if the time comes and five are needed, the gods ought to be satisfied with those four—plus Ogonooroo himself! I've been telling you ever since the swamp that you ought to be head chief of Opar, instead of Ogonooroo. He's old and fat, you're strong and powerful. Now's the time to strike! You get rid of him and tell the people that the gods commanded you to sacrifice him, that you're their new leader. I'll back you with my rifle. Then when things quiet down, I get my ivory. Next year I'll be back, with five whites for you. Agreed?"

Waziru chewed his lip, considering. And he suddenly nodded. "Yes! Then when Tarzan is captured I will spill his blood myself—and not as a sacrifice!"

So now the reason for Waziru's behavior was explained. Hawkins had been nudging him to revolt against Ogonooroo. Waziru, tempted, had been turning it over in his mind; he had reached his decision.

The two men left the cave and it became wholly dark. Tarzan backed hurriedly into the open, to watch with Chetah as the procession wended past below, on its way to the place of sacrifice.

Clouds still veiled the moon, but they were drifting away. Whatever Tarzan was to do, it had to be done soon.

And he had no idea as to what his next move would be.

Chapter 17   Night of the Blood Moon

The chanting rose in volume as the white prisoners were dragged up the mound. The booming of the ceremonial drum grew louder. The people there were working themselves up to a pitch of frenzy.

Tarzan descended the steps between the gigantic statues. He seemed to be entirely alone at this end of Opar, moving along below the huts piled up one on top of another against the great cliff.

Chetah trotted along beside him, shivering from the cold. Tarzan felt coldness, also, but of a different sort. Dark figures were moving about on the mound, and he knew what they were doing. The Penrods, Camage Dean, and Fletcher were being bound to those sacrificial racks.

He cudgeled his brain for some move that would free them. No plan came to him. That plot by Hawkins and

265

Waziru against Ogonooroo might be turned against those two—but how?

Tarzan came to what seemed to be a town square. He encountered, first, a deep, narrow hole that he skirted with an angry frown. It was the pit of skulls, of which he had heard so much, another symbol of the barbaric cruelty of this place.

Then he discovered something else: a low platform with a drum on it, set flat, peeled rhino hide stretched tightly over a round frame. Something, Tarzan thought, that was probably used to summon people to hear announcements. He studied the drum, then turned for a glance at the towering dwellings of Opar, his brain beginning to work very fast.

Chetah muttered complainingly, shivering harder. Tarzan murmured, "Perhaps you will be warm soon."

Then he plucked Dick Penrod's cigarette lighter from under his leopard skin, where it had been ever since he had found it on the trail.

Hawkins and Waziru had used fire as a weapon against him. Tarzan meant now to use it against them.

He knelt beside Chetah. "Little one, listen to me as you have never listened before!" Tarzan said. "Take the flame-

maker. Go with it to those huts you see. Burn them! Touch
fire to wood everywhere, quickly!"

Chetah stared at the lighter, brow wrinkling. She chirped
in agitated protest. Tarzan had told her at the lake that
burning things was bad. She reminded him of it earnestly.

"I know I told you that then," Tarzan said. "But I am
telling you another thing now! Do as I say. Burn everything! Go and do it at once!"

He put the lighter in her hand. She snapped it, fire
spurted, and Chetah hurriedly blew it out. She whimpered,
anticipating that she would now be told she was bad for
having made the fire.

"It is all right; that is what I want you to do," Tarzan
said. He gave her a shove. "Hurry!"

Chetah left him, going at a slow and reluctant pace
toward the huts. It was hard to tell how much she had
understood of his words. There were times when Chetah
showed a remarkable grasp of complicated instructions,
and times when she either could not, or would not, comprehend the simplest things.

Tarzan leaped up to the drum platform. He had to trust
Chetah would work out in her mind what she must do,
and then do it.

He struck the rhino hide lightly with his fist, and produced a sharp, twanging sound. Then he beat out Ogonooroo's call, making it hurried and urgent, twice repeated.

The roar of the crowd at the place of sacrifice, the booming of the ceremonial drum, were both silenced. The moon was appearing, bright and almost full.

Tarzan quickly began to send a message. "This is Omoru. I have caught the white man that I was ordered to trap and bring to the place of sacrifice."

It was hard to send "Omoru." What Tarzan actually beat out on the drum was a combination of sounds that meant "strong warrior." It was understood. He heard a relieved yell from Josiah Hawkins. Then the throng yonder began to hum like a hive of wild bees, with excited talk about this turn of events.

Another yell came from the bridge—one of the guards there, who knew no one had crossed from the far side of the canyon. Tarzan's fist beat against rhino hide again: "I have squeezed the ribs of the white man, and he has told me many things to save himself. He and the white with the gun have plotted together to burn Opar and seize the ivory. They were set to do this by Waziru, who plans to kill the great chief, Ogonooroo."

Startled cries and shouts of anger now came from the crowd that pressed close to the mound where those five racks stood. A struggling, milling movement began there. Fights were breaking out. Hawkins yelled again and fired a shot from his rifle.

From the corner of his eye, Tarzan saw a bright flare of flame suddenly shoot up among the high-piled dwellings of Opar. Chetah had understood. She was doing as he had asked. Another pillar of fire leaped high in the air, spreading swiftly.

Tarzan risked a quick glance in that direction and saw Chetah on the move there, pausing to snap the lighter and start still another fire. Those dwellings, stacked on top of each other, would serve as natural flues, drawing the flames upward.

Footsteps pounded toward Tarzan; an arrow whistled close to his face. He went sideways off the platform and crouched a moment, using it as a shield. One of the bridge guards pounded around it, searching for him. Tarzan reached out, grabbed the man's legs and clamped them together, then lifted him, swung him at the platform as though he were a club, and threw him aside. The Oparian sprawled in the dirt on his face, all his senses momentarily beaten out of him by the attack.

Tarzan ran then, slanting toward the canyon edge and heading southward when he reached it. As he ran, he filled his lungs and sent a mighty shout at the milling crowd: "People of Opar! Your city is burning!"

Chetah was coming to join him, lighter in one hand, still tenaciously clinging to her bindle with the other.

The crowd was beginning to break up, with people rushing to save their homes, their belongings. It was a movement that became a panic-stricken rout, a dark flood pouring from the place of sacrifice back to the high cliff where a dozen fires flared now.

Tarzan heard the voice of Waziru bellowing orders in that mob, heard the fierce shouts of men battling each other—the warriors loyal to Waziru struggling with those who fought for Ogonooroo.

It was a scene of wild confusion, which was what Tarzan had hoped for, what he had planned to achieve. He had turned the thoughts of all of them away from the sacrifices, had forced Waziru and Hawkins to fight for their lives. And it had to continue for a few moments longer.

Tarzan went up the sacrificial mound from the canyon side. It was a place brightly lighted by the sheets of flame

spreading across the cliff half a mile away.

No one came to oppose him. The mound itself was deserted, and so was the space all around it, though some bodies were sprawled on the ground, trampled in that panicky rush or struck down in the fighting that had accompanied it.

The four he sought were bound to the sacrificial racks, their arms outstretched, wrists tied to the crossbars that topped them. Penrod turned his head. "Tarzan!" he croaked in thanksgiving. Then, "Free the women first—"

Tarzan shook his head, slashing knife blade through the bonds that held Penrod's wrists. "I may need your help. Go and get us some spears. There are several lying about on the ground."

Penrod hurried to obey, rubbing his wrists to restore circulation to them. Tarzan freed Camage Dean next, then Diana Penrod, who swayed but shook her head as both Camage and Tarzan put out hands to support her.

"I'll be all right," Diana said. "I've been weak, leaning on people, long enough. Tarzan, what do you want us to do?"

Penrod was back with two spears. Chetah was jumping about in great excitement, bindle bouncing, waving the lighter and trying to tell of the part she had played in all this.

Fletcher was jerking at his bonds and crying out hysterically: "Don't leave me here! You couldn't do a thing like that!"

"Keep quiet!" Tarzan said, and cut him free.

A shuddering wail sounded in the night: "Ogonooroo is no more!"

Then a chant that quickly swelled in volume: "Waziru is now great chief of Opar! Hail, Waziru!"

Hawkins and Waziru had achieved their objective. With Ogonooroo out of the way the fighting would probably soon be ended, and the search for the one responsible for those fires would begin. Tarzan said, "We'll head at once for the bridge. Penrod, give me one of the spears. I'll go first. You bring up the rear. We may be attacked along the way—"

That was when Diana suddenly cried out and took a staggering step toward him, arm outstretched. She would have fallen if Tarzan had not reached out quickly to support her. "My arm!" she gasped. "It feels as though it's —burning—"

By the eerie glow of flaming Opar he saw a spider on

Diana's bare arm, between elbow and shoulder. Tarzan stared in sheer disbelief. He reached out to flick it off, saw the flash of red from its underside.

Karwee. But the deadly spider was never found in mountain country. . . . Then Tarzan remembered the bindle of Chetah, who had been standing beside Diana a moment ago, and he understood. Karwee had been in that bindle ever since the swamp, dormant and sluggish as they moved into the high, cold country, stirring to life with the burning heat here, choosing this moment of all moments to emerge and leap to living flesh and bite deeply.

Diana was sagging in Tarzan's grasp. He lowered her gently to the ground, then made the crisscross cuts, lightning flicks of his knife, to make the blood flow.

He sucked that blood and the poison mingled with it, then turned his head for a second to Camage. "Miss Dean! Make a tourniquet. Tie it just below her shoulder."

That was to keep the poison from reaching Diana's heart. Camage obeyed, moving quickly. Chetah huddled on the ground, moaning; she knew that this was all somehow connected with her bindle.

Penrod knelt to take his wife's hand. Diana's eyes were open. She spoke, voice weak and thready: "Go on—without me. Leave me here. And, Dick, I'm sorry for—everything—"

Dick Penrod bit his lip hard. "You others can go ahead. There's still a chance for you to escape. I'll stay with her."

Tarzan gave him a glance. "I think we may have acted in time. And she goes with us."

He continued to work methodically, doing all that could be done. The precious seconds flew. They could have reached the bridge by now, could have been across it.

Diana's eyes were closed. She was unconscious, in shock. Tarzan lifted the woman and slung her over his left shoulder. "You'll have to lead out, Penrod. Let's start."

Fletcher, who had been standing nervously by, shaking with fright, began to run, going ahead of them.

Tarzan moved at a steady pace, spear in his right hand, Camage beside him. He looked back, speaking to Chetah, "Come on!"

Chetah lifted her bindle automatically, then suddenly dropped it with a bitter grimace and hurried along beside him, leaving it behind, abandoned.

Fire covered the whole face of the great cliff now, with flaming brands flying far through the air. A tense exclamation came from Penrod: "The bridge is burning!"

Tarzan had already seen this. One of the great timber uprights that anchored the structure on this side of the canyon had become a flaming torch, and fire was gnawing at the ropes supporting the footpath. He moved faster.

They were skirting the edge of the canyon. No one was guarding the bridge. Fletcher, running ahead, darted out onto it and began to make his way across. It was swaying violently, probably shaken by air currents set in motion by the fire.

Penrod reached the bridge. The air had become very hot. Sparks showered around them. Camage cried out and beat at her smoking skirt. Tarzan handed over Diana to her husband.

"Miss Dean, go first," he said. "Penrod, follow her. I'll wait here until you're on the other side."

He had an eye on those burning ropes. This end of the bridge was liable to fall at any second.

They started across. Then—angry shouts, men rushing at Tarzan, spears flashing and the hiss of arrows. Their flight had been discovered.

Tarzan threw the spear he held. An Oparian sank down, crying out, impaled by it. Tarzan leaped about, quickly, coolly, near the bridge, dodging their weapons, catching another spear out of the air with a flick of his hand and hurling it back with unerring accuracy, holding them off.

Some of these warriors trying to bring him down had been at the crocodile river. They remembered his prowess there and cried out fearfully, drawing back. Perhaps, Tarzan thought, he had a chance to run for it before the bridge fell.

Then—there came a furious bellow of rage; through swirling smoke he saw Waziru coming at him.

The scar-faced chieftain had a spear with a long, sharp blade, like a knife, instead of a point. He drove it low at Tarzan, slashing at his legs.

Tarzan leaped back, snatching another spear from the air, and parried Waziru's blow with that. Beyond the new great chief of Opar he saw Hawkins, who was trying to get a clear shot at him with his rifle.

Waziru swung that sharp blade. It cut clear through the tough wooden haft of Tarzan's spear, leaving him weaponless. Waziru shouted in triumph, rushing him.

Tarzan waited, iron-nerved, as he had waited for the rhino's charge that night in the jungle—waited until Waziru's spear blade was only an inch, if that, from his body. Then Tarzan whipped aside, a move too fast for anyone to follow. And Waziru could not stop his rush. He screamed, feet suddenly treading on empty air as he went over the canyon edge—a long scream that was abruptly chopped off short as he plummeted into the depths of the canyon.

Tarzan was still moving. He leaped at Hawkins, gripped the rifle, and backed up fast, dragging the man with him onto the bridge.

Hawkins fought to break away, swing the rifle and pull trigger at Tarzan. He managed to get off a shot, a whip-lashing explosion in Tarzan's face. Tarzan held on, dragging him still, using the man as a shield. Some Oparians ventured onto the bridge after him, then turned and scrambled hurriedly back.

The whole bridge structure was sagging, beginning to sink. Hawkins screamed in sudden frantic fear, letting the rifle go and clawing at Tarzan. "I'll go with you—do anything you say—only save me!"

"Hang on!" Tarzan gripped his arm and turned, leaping to seize a rope.

The bridge fell, a tangle of ropes and falling planks, swinging like a pendulum toward the far canyon wall, where the supports still held. Tarzan rode with it, holding fast to Hawkins. But the man struggled in hysteria, still screaming, writhing and twisting. The loose cloth of his jacket slipped between Tarzan's fingers. He tightened his grip, to no avail; the cloth tore away and Hawkins was gone, following Waziru into the depths below.

Tarzan hung on, and took the battering shock as he hit the opposite canyon wall. He looked down at the blackness beneath him for a moment, regretting that he could not have saved Hawkins and delivered the man to justice for his many wicked deeds. But perhaps justice had caught up with Hawkins after all.

Not until then did Tarzan discover that Chetah had made the wild flight through space with him. She was chattering excitedly. Chetah wanted to do it again.

Tarzan snorted. "I thought you had crossed with the others! Come on, let's join them."

They climbed together up the web of ropes that was still anchored to this side of the canyon. Across the canyon, Opar burned brightly in the night; perhaps justice had overtaken that place of evil, also, cleansing it with fire.

Five days later they all stood together on the bank of the broad, placid Ngamu, with some hippos snorting and splashing in the near distance. A plume of black smoke showed above the water. It was a boat, bound down-river, that was heading this way.

Dick Penrod cleared his throat. "Well . . ."

Tarzan smiled. "Good-bys are always awkward, so let's not say them. Instead, we'll hope to meet again some day."

Two of those five days had been spent waiting on Diana's recovery. Then they had moved on by easy stages, through the mountains by the pass and down to the Ngamu.

Tarzan studied them now. Dick Penrod stood quietly, steady and resolute. He had found himself during the long ordeal—would return to flying, he had told Tarzan, with the Navy again if it would have him.

Diana was in full agreement. "When I remember how I made Dick do what I wanted, drifting around the world, accomplishing nothing, instead of adjusting my life to his, I—I feel a little sick," she said. "But that's all behind me forever!"

Her shallowness and petty selfishness were gone. And her heroism, after Karwee's bite, had paid for all that. She was a better person as a result of all she had been forced to endure.

Camage Dean, slim and tanned, had benefited also. "I

shall live my own life after this," she said, taking Tarzan's hand. "I'll never be dependent on anybody again."

As for Hal Fletcher, standing sullenly apart—well, he was one of those who would never change, who would never benefit from any experience. He would return to civilization unchanged, the same worthless leech that he had been before. And Tarzan, a little sad, reluctant to see the others go, was heartily glad to be seeing the last of Hal Fletcher.

He spoke to Chetah, "Time for us to be moving along."

She shook hands gravely with the Penrods, with Camage Dean. Chetah had been rather moody since Opar, and even the prospect of seeing her friends, the forest chimps along the Ruwenzori, did not cheer her up. She was remembering that beautiful metal ring, abandoned on the night of fire.

Penrod suddenly snapped his fingers. "I almost forgot, Chetah; I have a present for you!" And he handed her his lighter.

She exclaimed with delight, holding it up to catch the sunlight. Chetah had never thought this would belong to her. It made everything all right once more.

Penrod winked at Tarzan. "I let most of the gas out of

it; she isn't likely to burn down that forest of yours!"

The boat was almost here. Tarzan and Chetah went to where a nearby belt of thick timber began, paused there a moment to lift their arms in farewell. Then:

"Up, little one!" Tarzan said.

Chetah sprang to his back, he leaped into the trees, and they were gone, a steady, swift pace through the high branches, heading westward.

Opar would still live on its high mountain shelf, but the savage rites of the blood moon would be performed no more. Its location was known now. Tarzan would report that, and Opar would be watched.

As for the fabulous hoard of ivory in the secret cave, he did not care in the slightest degree what became of that.

Others could struggle for treasure if they wished. Gripping a liana, swinging at a dizzying sweep through space, far above the earth, Chetah squealing gleefully, Tarzan smiled in contentment.

This was all he wanted, or ever would want—the wild, free life, the long miles of Africa spinning past, a warm wind in his face.

And some new adventure, waiting beyond the far horizon. Tarzan moved even faster.

Whitman CLASSICS

Mrs. Wiggs of the Cabbage Patch	The Little Lame Prince
Little Women	Robin Hood
Black Beauty	The Wonderful Wizard of Oz
Huckleberry Finn	Robinson Crusoe
Heidi	Wild Animals I Have Known
The Call of the Wild	
Tom Sawyer	The War of the Worlds

Here are some of the best-loved stories of all time. Delightful...intriguing...never-to-be-forgotten tales that you will read again and again. Start your own home library of WHITMAN CLASSICS so that you'll always have exciting books at your fingertips.

Whitman ADVENTURE and MYSTERY Books

Adventure Stories for GIRLS and BOYS...

TIMBER TRAIL RIDERS
The Long Trail North
The Texas Tenderfoot
The Luck of Black Diamond
Mystery of the Hollywood Horse
The Mysterious Dude

POWER BOYS SERIES
The Haunted Skyscraper
The Flying Skeleton
The Million-Dollar Penny
The Burning Ocean

DONNA PARKER
In Hollywood
At Cherrydale
Special Agent
On Her Own
A Spring to Remember
Mystery at Arawak
Takes a Giant Step

TROY NESBIT SERIES
Sand Dune Pony
Indian Mummy Mystery
Mystery at Rustlers' Fort

New Stories About Your Television Favorites...

Dr. Kildare
The Magic Key

Lassie
Secret of the Summer
Forbidden Valley

The Munsters
The Great Camera Caper

Combat! The Counterattack

Walt Disney's Annette
Mystery at Smugglers' Cove
Desert Inn Mystery
Mystery at Medicine Wheel

Voyage to the Bottom of the Sea

The Beverly Hillbillies

Introducing an Exciting New Series

ROBIN KANE
The Mystery of the Blue Pelican
The Mystery of the Phantom